HIGH STAKES
by
Joel Betancourt

All rights reserved

All characters, names and incidents depicted in this book are either a product of the author's imagination or have been used fictitiously. Any resemblance to actual events, locales or persons, living or dead, is entirely coincidental.

This book is a copyright protected work. No part of this manuscript can be reproduced in any way without the permission of the author. This includes the work as a whole or any part of the publication.

Copyright © 2012 by Joel Betancourt

Cover design by Melaine Ann Schweighardt

Praise for High Stakes

"Joel Betancourt's writing is dazzling ... brilliant. You've heard the phrase "a short, sharp shock?" ... Well, that describes these stories perfectly. Sharp dialog and surprising, even shocking plots (many of which deal with heart-breaking loss) make this collection a fantastic read. Betancourt's a powerful new voice in fiction of the weird and fantastic."

—Rick Hautala
Author of *Occasional Demons* and *Indian Summer*

"I have a confession to make.

I published Joel Betancourt's story "The Painter" – about an artist and his obsession– in Horror Garage magazine because I just couldn't get it out of my head. Seriously. To the degree that I considered Betancourt may have actually stabbed me in the cranium with a screwdriver and pried open my skull. Gently.

This collection of Joel's work provides many other stories to obsess on. There are werewolves, ghosts and monsters. There is life, death, and in-between. Betancourt is especially adept at subtly bending the reader's mind, using words that flow like smooth jazz to uncover parts of human nature hidden in the shadows – you might just recognize yourself blowin' the sax in purgatory.

Oh, and "The Painter"? That's here too, and it's still as devastating as when I first read it."
—Pitch Black
Editor and publisher of *Horror Garage*

"Betancourt's short works appear to emanate from a dark, fevered mind. A soul saving fisherman, legendary werewolves and psychotic disorders, are just a random sample of what is sure to keep the reader awake each night. Already well known for his Horror, this collection of tales display the depth and diversity of his talent. Bolt the doors and lock the windows."
—Graeme Johns
Author of *Immortal Desire* and *Situation Sabotage*

"Betancourt has compiled an excellent collection of stories in High Stakes … His stories make you stop and think … I highly recommend this collection."
—Colleen Wanglund
Reviewer for *The Horror Fiction Review*

Dedication

When I was a boy my father told me that the best friend a man could have is a book. It's taken me the better part of my life to realize that the best friend a boy could have is a father. We rarely saw eye to eye on most subjects and we argued more times than I'd care to remember but in the end, I am my father's son and I wouldn't have it any other way.

To my father, Mario D. Betancourt.

Forward

What defines you? On the road of life, what shapes your soul? Is it the people one encounters? Maybe. The paths we diverge from? Possibly. What are the top three experiences that transform you, transport you or define you as a traveler? For me, it's love, fear and family. This collection of short stories takes you to the places that have shaped my core. Many of the tales deal with at least one or more of these subjects. I hope you enjoy them.

Joel Betancourt

Contents

Of Wolves and Moons	9
The Painter	14
Waiting	20
Splitting Up	23
The Meeting	41
Found Note	46
Occupation	48
666	57
Journal Found in Woods	60
The Writers Group	63
The Last Song	66
A Father's Warning	75
Getting Personal	77
The Fisherman	82
High Stakes	106
Passed Out	115
As Promised	116
Charlie's Invitation	120
Found Doll	124
The Letter	138
Last Bullet	143
The Tree	144
Lostinhorrorhouse.com	157
Recovered	161
No Pain	173
Divided	191
Lost Pup	200
Afterward	208
About the Author	219
Note to Reader	221

HIGH STAKES

Of Wolves and Moons

"Why does the wolf howl, daddy?" my boy asked as we walked past the forest and back to our farm.

I ran my fingers through the dark strands of his hair. The soft locks reminded me of his mother. He looked up at me with eyes filled with wonder. The silver necklace that hugged his neck bounced moonbeams as bright as his innocence. The medallion of St. Lazarus his mother had given him years ago swung near his heart.

"The wolf howls because he misses her, my son,"

"Who? Who does the wolf miss?"

I listened closely to the night. Crickets chirped from hidden corners of the forest. Small animals scurried through piles of dead leaves. I waited for the mournful wail. The wolf's cry crept through the night air, crawled through my ears, and into my memories.

"He's lonely. He misses his female wolf."

"Why does he miss her?"

"She's gone. Hunters … hunters took her away from him. With their bullets and guns and lies. They stole her away."

"Is he sad, daddy?"

"Yes."

The howl came again. I looked up into the sky. A half-moon frowned down upon me. I opened the door to our farmhouse. We entered and I locked the moon out behind me.

"Why does he howl at the moon?" my boy asked.

"For answers. He wants to know why she's gone."
"Does the moon ever answer?"
"No."
"Why does he howl then?"
"He hopes that one day the moon will answer him."

I tucked my boy into his bed and kissed his forehead. I hoped he'd dream of bicycles, of other children, and of summer days lost in the joys of youth. I hoped he did not dream of wolves and I prayed that he definitely would not dream of moons.

~ * ~

"Daddy, daddy," my boy said as he shook me from my empty dreams. "The howls are louder tonight."

I sat up in bed, glanced out the window and saw the moon. This time it stared back at me three quarters full.

The wolf's cries came again. They stole the sounds of the forest, leaving only the wail to rise in pitch as if the sound could touch the moon.

"Yes, they are louder," I whispered. The newly broken sleep strangled my voice.

I placed my hand on my son's shoulder. The silver necklace touched my skin and I remembered his mother, her eyes as dark and deep as the twilight hours that filled my life with longing so many years ago. Her hair, dark and full with strands that rested gently on her breasts. I thought of her breasts and how they had quenched my desire through those twilight hours.

"You must sleep, my boy. You must sleep and dream, and not listen to the howls."

"They keep me up."

"You must try."

I walked him to his room, sat on the side of his bed and pulled the covers up to his neck. "Sleep. Tomorrow I will take you into town and we will go to the ice cream shop. You can have as many scoops as you like. Then we will stay in the park as long as you like. You will play with other children. We will stay there until your legs tire of running and your heart tires of laughing and then we will come home. Would you like that?"

"Yes daddy, I would."

I kissed him on the forehead and squeezed his hand. "Good night then."

~ * ~

The next day I walked my boy through town. We spoke of bugs, and school, and birthday presents. We had ice cream and soda and I smiled as he played on the swings in the park. I laughed as he fell into the sandbox to joke with the other children. I sat still under the bright sky and forgot about wolves and moons and wives and little boys who will never know their mothers.

~ * ~

"Daddy, daddy, are you okay?"

I awoke. Fever filled my body and I could feel my bones breaking. The night air suffocated me.

I looked at my son. "Yes ... yes..."

"I heard the howling. I wanted to see if you were okay," he said.

"Yes—"

Pain surged through my soul. I reeled as agony tore at my limbs.

"It's okay daddy. It's okay," my boy said as he held my hand. I glanced at him. His necklace was gone.

"What happened to the—"

"It broke. It broke in the park," he replied.

"Did you lose it?"

"No, it's in my room. I still have it but I can't wear it."

"Your mother ... your mother gave that to you when you were a baby. You need—"

The pain broke my body.

"It's okay, daddy. It's okay."

My limbs stretched. My teeth grew under my shattered jaw. My body twisted and grew.

"You'll be okay, daddy," my son repeated. He patted my head.

I rolled over. My spine stretched my torso so that I spanned the length of the bed. My new body grew its hair. My hands twisted into paws. My mouth lengthened.

"It's okay," he said.

I looked at my son with sad eyes. He took hold of me behind my head and led me off the bed by my neck. I crawled through our house. My claws scratched the wooden floor as my little boy guided me outside.

The night held a full moon larger than I had seen in years. A hunter's moon. It was there when I crawled through the field and into the forest. It was there when I cried, there when I howled and it was there when I asked the moon the questions I have always asked.

This time I hoped, no, I prayed, that the moon would answer me.

The Painter

Paint-splattered sheets engulfed Julian Michael Baiulo as he dreamt. He slept more these days. The dreams were bad. Nightmares of life. And occasionally, nightmares of nothing. Just the pain that filled him. He grappled against the worn linen sheets as his head filled with colored paintings of his life.

A knock echoed in the empty apartment.

Julian shook. The mattress he slept on trembled with him. More cotton stuffing broke from the corner of his bed.

Knock.

"Wharrr..." The sound came from Julian's chest.

Knock, knock.

"Ahh ... what?" Julian's eyes peeked from under the covers.

Knock, knock, knock.

The door, thought Julian. *She's here*. He peeled the sheets off his body.

"Come ... come in," said Julian.

The door opened. Helen came in wearing a full-length black dress. She looked over the apartment. Aside from the mattress, Julian, and several crushed tubes of paint, the apartment was naked.

"I didn't think you'd come so soon," said Julian. He looked at his dirty hands. He let the sleeves of his shirt flap over the backs of his hands. "Look at me. I must be a mess." He folded his hands under his arms.

"You're fine," replied Helen. A single cut of hair swayed from behind her ear to her cheek. Julian watched the black strand as it kissed her porcelain skin.

"I'm sorry, not that many people stop by anymore," said Julian.

Helen looked around the room. Small pieces of trash hid in corners. Crumpled papers, plastic bags, and a few slices of broken glass huddled together against walls of peeling paint. They all seemed to flee from something that hung on the wall. A painting. A concealed painting.

"Look at you. Just look," said Julian.

Helen kept her eyes on the painting. It was covered by a large white cloth.

"Is this it?" she asked.

"Oh, yeah. That's it."

"May I?" Helen reached for a corner of the white sheet.

"Wait, no ... I ... I don't want you to look just yet." Julian stared at her. "I just wanted ... I was thinking. I haven't seen it in natural light. I got so used to working by candle light that I don't even know what it might look like in the day."

"Is it another one of me?"

"Yes. You ... you're a hard ghost to shake."

"Am I? Am I, Julian?" She looked into his eyes.

Julian turned away.

"I thought you said it was over," said Helen. "I thought you told me, never again."

"It's not that easy for me. You might ... you might have forgotten me but—"

"But what, Julian?"

"But how can I forget you?"

"Isn't that what you wanted, Julian? To forget me."

Julian's mouth trembled softy, "Yes."

"What?"

"Yeah. I wanted to forget you."

"And?"

"Why do you do this? Why? Does this get you high? Knowing how much I need you and you ... you being able to destroy me so easily. Is that it? That's the thrill. It is, isn't it?"

Their eyes locked.

"You called me, didn't you," said Helen.

"Yes." Julian broke from her stare and walked toward the painting. "You know, no one buys my work. Not anymore. I don't even recall the last time I sold a painting." He glanced out his apartment window. Small fragments of life outside called to him. The life of the city. "It's funny, I can still remember when all of New York wanted me. When I was not only the talk of the town, I was the town. The art world revolved around me. All the critics wrote about me. Me and only me."

Helen turned. Her stiletto heels nipped at the wooden floor as she made her way toward the door.

"I'm leaving Julian."

"Why couldn't you love me?"

"Don't." She turned to face him.

"Fucking Christ, look at you! Just look. I made you beautiful. Me, my paintings made you gorgeous. All those painting I did of you. It was me." Julian grabbed her arm. His fingers wrenched around her bicep. "And I'm nothing to you."

"Stop..."

"Why, why, when I gave you so much? When I gave you everything."

Helen tried to pull away from his grip. "Julian, please."

"I made you. I made you breathtaking. A hideous monster like you ... beautiful."

"Julian."

"And look at me. Look ... Look!"

She tried to yank free.

His grip dug deeper.

She looked into his eyes. "Yes."

"I'm dying." His grip released. His fingers slid off of her. Julian made his way to the dirty mattress on the floor, sat down, and covered himself with the sheets. "Why? Do you even feel anything?"

"No."

"Why?"

"Julian, you're the one who always called on me."

He sat frozen.

"Would you like me to leave?" she asked.

"Wait ... I ... I don't want you to go."

"What do you want?"

"Stay, please ... you ... you haven't seen the painting yet. Please. Please, I'm sorry. I didn't mean ... I need you in my arms again. Please, let's just forget. Let's forget everything. Okay?"

"Okay."

"I need you."

"I know." Helen walked toward him. Her right hand pulled the strap of her dress off of her shoulder. Her left hand released the other strap. The dress dropped to the floor.

Julian looked at her body, at her white skin. Porcelain. "Wait, the painting."

Helen walked to the covered painting. She reached for the corner of the sheet and pulled. The cloth fell beside her dress.

She stared at Julian Michael Baiulo's latest masterpiece. Rough, crude and jagged brush marks ripped at the canvas. The colors, dark and cold incased an image. An image of her. An image of him. The painting—a close up of his right bicep strangled by a rubber hose, the fingers in his left hand pushing a needle into a swollen vein.

"It's both of us, together," said Helen.

"Yes."

She turned toward him. Her heels clicked. "My sweet little junkie."

She pulled the sheets off of him. Her body slid down to meet his.

"Why did I fall in love with you?" he asked.

"Shhhh ..."

"Wait, this ... this time, afterward ... I ... I don't want to wake up." Julian rolled up his sleeves and took Helen into his arms one last time.

Waiting

Do I hold on too tightly? Ashley thinks so. All I know is that from the moment I saw her, I wanted her.

I still remember the first time I laid eyes on her. I was walking by Florida Atlantic University's library and, as I passed the study hall, I caught a glimpse of a beautiful blonde with the most serious look on her face. She was leaning over a textbook, lost in thought. I paused long enough for her to notice me. When she looked up, I froze. Then, she smiled. That smile has haunted me to this day.

I walked past her, afraid to say anything. I felt like such a wimp.

Later that night, I couldn't help replaying our encounter in my head over and over again. I should have said something. I should have told her anything that came to mind. It couldn't have been worse than running off the way I did.

I couldn't sleep that night. I swore I'd find her and at least introduce myself.

I spent my lunch hours in that exact spot every day for a week. Between classes, I'd pass by the study hall. If anyone needed something from another class, I'd volunteer to get it with the hope of finding the blonde with the unforgettable smile.

When it was time to hit the books, I camped out in the study hall. I even declined when my roommate asked me to hit one of the local bars with him on Friday night. Knowing my plans, he told me, "She'd better be worth the wait."

One week later, my patience paid off. She returned to the same spot, and I finally introduced myself. I haven't left her side since.

We dated for six months before I proposed. The wedding was scheduled for the summer following graduation, but the accident postponed everything.

~ * ~

Ashley has these great quirks. These little imperfections that make her perfect. She misplaces things—keys, money, her purse. I usually find them and return them to our dresser for her. It upsets her from time to time. I don't know why. It's just my way of showing that I still love her.

She'll fall asleep on the couch most nights. Sometimes reading a book or a magazine. It's one of the little habits that make her endearing. I'll take her glasses off and remove the book from her lap and set them down on the coffee table for her.

Once, I picked her up and tucked her into bed but that really scared her. I guess she didn't remember moving from the couch and it spooked her. I don't like to see her upset so I promised I wouldn't do that again.

~ * ~

Ashley doesn't smile like before. It's rare now. Ever since the accident.

After the crash, she would cry and cry. I hated watching her like that. It was a month before it stopped.

She still blames herself but I urge her not to. A tire blew out at the wrong time and at the wrong place, that's all. I keep telling her that but she doesn't hear me.

It's been a while now. I don't see her smile like before. I guess it's difficult.

I try not to upset her. I know she still feels responsible. Ever since the funeral, I keep trying to tell her that it wasn't her fault. That I still love her. That it's going to be all right. I know she can't hear me but I do it anyway. I'm waiting for the day that she'll hear me and see me again.

What can I say? She's worth the wait.

Splitting Up

Steven Harrison sat frozen in his chair, the furniture around him spun. Only the rocks glass in his hand kept him anchored. Half a sip of scotch was left in the cup.

"Look at you," said Adam.

The room stopped spinning. Steven glanced up.

"Look at you," Adam repeated. "You're just going to sit there, aren't you?

"Maybe," Steven said.

"Maybe? Maybe, my ass. God, you can be a real pussy, can't you?"

Steven chuckled.

"Yep, you sure can," Adam replied. "You're just going to stay home and feel sorry for yourself."

"As opposed to?"

"As opposed to growing some balls and getting out there."

"Like you?" Steven pointed at Adam with his drink.

"What the fuck does that mean?"

"Nothing." Steven lowered his glass.

"Yeah, that's what I thought." Adam turned away. He found a small mirror hanging on the wall and took note of his features, combed his hair with his fingers and checked out his smile. "You know, Amy's out there."

"Yeah," Steven said.

Adam turned back toward Steven. "And we're in here. No good, boss."

"What do you want me to do?"

Adam shrugged his shoulders. "You going to stay locked up in here the whole night? Cause I'd like to be with Amy."

"I don't know."

"Well, how about worrying about that later. This room is always going to be here."

"And there's always going to be another Amy."

"Not if you keep this up," Adam said.

"What do you want me to do?"

"Try and block some of this shit out. At least tonight and allow me—"

"Allow you to block it out your own way," Steven said.

"It hasn't bothered you before."

"Do you know what tonight is?" Steven asked.

"Don't start."

"Do you?"

"No, Steve, I haven't a fucking clue. Cocksucker."

"It's October seventh."

"Yes, Steven. It's the seventh. Fucking Christ. Welcome to Steven's pity party. Leave all hope at the door. It's feel sorry for one's self at the Harrison house tonight."

"It's not like that."

"No Steven? What the fuck is it like, then?"

"It's not like that and you know it."

"Kiss Amy's ass good-bye, cause I got to deal with this shit. Damn, it was going so well with her. You know that?" Adam paced around the room. "You want to start this shit? You get rid of her."

"What do you want me to do?" Steven rose from his chair.

"I don't know." Adam snuck in behind him and slumped down into the seat. "Why don't you try the 'my wife's dead' bit? That seems to always work. Fuck, get rid of her. You killed it for me."

"You're not going to tell her anything?"

"No, Steven, it's going to have to be you, this time."

"You're kidding me?"

"Look at my face. Do I look like I'm kidding? Go out there and break it to her cause I'm sure as hell not going to."

"But she's your date."

"Not anymore. You're my date now. So, get rid of her."

Steven paused, not quite believing Adam.

"Go on my love." Adam said with a forced smile. "It's our night tonight."

Steven left.

Adam stared around the room. The old guest bedroom had been turned into an office. Over the years, it became more of a waiting room.

Steven returned. "She's gone."

"Great. Another loving night alone with you. As cute as you are, Steven, Amy would have been a better partner. At least, in bed.

"We met on this day. I can't believe it's been so many years since—"

"Don't start this shit," Adam interrupted.

"We met on this day."

"Cut it the fuck loose! She's gone. She left and there's nothing you or I can do about it."

"Why do you refuse to call her by her name?"

"Because she's gone. You want to forget something, you put it out of your mind."

"How?" Steven asked.

Adam stood and paced around the room. "Any way you can."

"And you? How do you do it?"

"Any way I can," Adam said.

"Amy?" Steven questioned.

"Yeah, Amy. That's one way. And it works."

"For a moment."

"At least then, it's worth it."

"Is it?"

"Yeah."

"I don't think so anymore," Steven said.

"No, you wouldn't."

"And neither do you," Steven said.

"Yes I do," Adam said.

"Then say her name."

"Fuck off."

"Say her name."

"Mrs. First name, fuck. Last name, off."

"Say her name."

"I just did. Oh, you want the full name. Mrs. Fuck Off Harrison. Are you happy? This shit's old. I'm tired of it," Adam said.

"You want it to stop?"

"Oh, could you? Pretty please?"

"Just tell me her name," Steven said.

"No."

"One name."

"No."

"Christina," Steven said.

"No."

"Christina."

"You fuck." Adam lunged at Steven, pinning him against the back wall. "You want me to say her name?"

"Yeah."

"Do you?" Adam trembled.

"Say it. Christina."

"Chri…" Adam started. His body, betrayed by emotions, began to break.

"Christina," Steven urged.

"Chris…" Adam's face filled with tears. "Fuck you."

"Christina," Steven replied.

"Chri … Christi. Christina," Adam said.

Christina emerged from the bedroom. "Steven, what are you doing?" she asked.

Steven pulled away from the wall. "Nothing. I was … I was just talking to…" He realized Adam had vanished. "Where'd he go?"

"You mean your little friend?" she asked. "I don't know. I have a feeling he doesn't like to see me."

"No. He doesn't even like to think about you."

"I never met him before."

"No, we became friends after you … afterward."

"Oh," she replied.

"Do you know what today is?"

"Yes. I know."

"I still remember it like it was yesterday," Steven said. "When we met, I…"

"I have to go, Steven."

"No. Wait, please." Steven dropped to his knees before Christina. "Don't. Don't go. Not now. It's our day today. We met for the first time and … please. I don't want to spend it alone."

"What about Amy?" Christina asked and then vanished.

"That … that's not fair. That's not fair, Christina."

Steven looked up to find Christina gone. "What happened?"

"You passed out." Adam said. He sat in the chair with a glass of scotch in his hand.

"What?" Steven asked.

"You passed out."

"That's never happened before.

~ * ~

Steven sat at his desk. A cluster of papers and folders were spread out before him. He covered his eyes with his hands and tried to soothe his headache by rubbing his temples with his fingertips. He glanced up and was surprised to find Adam sitting in the chair in front of him. "Christ, what are you doing here?"

"Looking at you," Adam replied.

"How'd you get in here?"

"I teleported." Adam smirked. "How's it feel, Steven?"

"What?"

"How's it feel to be a cog in a broken machine?"

"Look, I have stuff to do."

"Oh yeah, I forgot." Mirroring the movements of a robot, Adam lifted his right arm and pretended to pass a piece of paper over to his left hand. He stamped the paper, turned his head from left to right, opened his eyes as wide as he could and, looked down at the imaginary sheet in front of him. He repeated the movement.

"You done?" Steven asked.

Adam mocked the voice of a robot. "No. Steven. I. Still. Have. More pa, pa, papers to file."

"Look I got…" Steven paused. "Christ, you've been drinking."

"No Steven. I have—"

"Don't give me that. I can smell it from here."

"Okay, Steven." Adam lifted his hands, palms up, toward Steven. "You got me. I have, so what?"

"I can't believe that…" Steven caught a glimpse of his boss, Mark Peppers, as he walked by his office. Peppers had his face planted into a folder, looking over notes.

"Harrison, you got the Anderson account?" Peppers paused finding something in his notes. "Ahh, Christ. I can't believe this." He turned around and stomped back toward the main office.

Steven looked at Adam. "Shit. You got to get out of here."

"What?" Adam asked.

"You've got to leave, now."

"Why? I can't talk to Peppers?"

"No."

"I got so many things I'd like to tell him."

"Yeah, we all would."

"No Steven. Not all of us."

"Well, I've got to work for a living."

"Yeah, but look at what you do? Look, look, look, look. Look at this little desk in this small office in this tiny world that Steven built."

"I like it here."

"No, you used to like it here."

"Go. Just go. If Peppers comes back, it's my ass."

"Why don't you tell him what you think of him?"

"Do me a favor and find a secretary's leg to hump or a fire hydrant to piss on, but just leave."

"Okay, but I was only trying to help."

"Go help someone else."

"Maybe I'll help Peppers." Adam walked out.

"Yeah, you go and—Shit." Steven ran after him but was stopped by Peppers outside his office.

"Damn idiots," Peppers mumbled. "Morons, the lot of them." Peppers turned toward Steven. "Harrison, you find the Anderson account?"

"I've been looking for it, sir."

"I didn't ask you to look for it. I asked you to get it."

"Yes, sir," Steven said.

"Well, get … have you been drinking?"

~ * ~

Adam sat in the center of Steven's home office. Slumped in the single chair, Adam took a mental inventory of the objects around him. Pieces of the life Steven had with Christina littered the room. Knick-knacks from vacations taken years ago, books that were never read peeked out from the bookshelf.

Steven entered the room.

Adam stood. "You're here early."

"Yeah, I got sent home."

"Why?"

"I don't want to talk about it," Steven said.

"Why not?"

"Peppers thought I was drinking."

Adam laughed.

"That's not funny," Steven said.

"Oh, sorry."

"What are you doing here anyway?"

"Nothing," Adam said.

"Don't you have hell to raise elsewhere?"

"No. No, I don't."

"I don't usually find you here."

"Yeah, I was just being a good house husband."

"In this room?" Steven asked.

"Yeah."

"You never come in here."

"Well, I just wanted to know what it was like to be you." Adam returned to the office chair and sat. "Just sit down in your favorite chair. And take a little stroll down memory lane."

"What's wrong?"

"Nothing," Adam replied.

"What's wrong?" Steven asked. The tone in his voice came across as a plea.

"Ahhh, fuck."

"What?"

"Amy."

"What about her?"

"Today, after I left the office. I stopped by to see her and…" Adam trailed off.

"And what? She didn't want to jump into bed with you and be your little sex slave?"

"She told me that she's fallen in love with me."

"Oh."

"Oh? Is that all you can say?" Adam asked.

"What else would you like me to say?"

"Nothing. You don't have to say a damn thing. Just stand there and look stupid." Adam threw his hands up in frustration. "Fuck."

"What are you going to do?" Steven asked.

"How should I know? You're the lovey dovey, lost romantic. Isn't this your department?" Adam looked away. "I didn't think that this would happen."

"What did you do?"

"What do you think I did? I smiled, kissed her gently and got the hell out of there."

"You just left her?" Steven asked.

"I didn't know what else to say or do."

"Oh, God."

"Wait, don't make me out to be the bad guy here. I had no intention of keeping this going any longer than it has. Okay? I just thought … I thought…"

"What?"

"I just thought that Amy was going to be like the rest," Adam said.

"What did you say?" Steven asked.

"You heard me."

"No. Apparently I didn't because I just thought I heard you say, you believed she was going to be like the others."

"Yeah," said Adam.

"What are you implying?"

"Nothing," Adam said.

"You're starting to fall for this girl."

"Stop it."

"You are. What the hell is wrong with you?" Steven asked.

"No, I'm not going to hear this shit from you."

"You better forget about her, cause it's not going to happen."

"Fuck off, Steven." Adam moved toward the door.

"Where are you going?"

"Somewhere that I won't have to listen to your bullshit." Adam slammed the door behind him.

~ * ~

Steven slept in the chair centered in his home office. His apartment was silent until Adam entered.

"Where have you been?" Steven asked.

"Out."

"Where?"

"I was out, Steven. I needed to get my head cleared. Is that okay with you?"

"Yeah."

"All right, if you don't mind, I'd like to get some rest."

"Wait."

"What now?" Adam asked, frustrated by the questioning.

"I was doing some thinking of my own and—"

"Oh God, here we go."

"Look, this thing with Amy, I've thought it over and you need to let her go."

"Is that what you've come up with?"

"Yes," Steven replied.

"Oh, well umm … look, this thing with your wife, I've been thinking, you need to let her go."

"Funny," Steven said.

"Is it?"

"Yeah."

"Well, I'm not trying to be funny," Adam said.

"No?"

"Nope."

"I don't think it's fair for—"

"For who?" Adam interrupted.

"It's not fair for her."

"Oh, for her."

"Yeah, it's only been—"

"It's been long enough."

"No."

"Let it go, Steven."

"No."

"Let it go," Adam said.

"How the fuck can you say that?"

"How can you not?"

"It's only been—"

"Long enough," Adam replied.

"No."

"You've got to let her go," Adam said.

"And you have?" Steven asked.

"What do you mean by that?" Adam asked.

"You can't even say her name."

"Maybe, I don't want to," Adam said.

"Maybe, you can't."

The phone rang, stopping both men. Steven answered. He spoke softly into the receiver. "Hello, Amy ... yes. Wait I don't think that would be a good idea."

"What is it?" Adam asked.

"She's coming over." Steven put down the receiver.

"What?"

"Is that where you went tonight?" Steven asked.

"Yeah."

"Great."

"I had to," Adam said.

"Yeah, sure."

"What do you want from me?"

"I want you to prove to me she's no longer inside you," Steven said.

"I have."

"How, by fucking everything that moves?"

"She's dead. She's gone and I'm here and you're still here. I do what I can to push her out of my mind. Life goes on, Steven. Death does not."

"You can't even admit that she was part of your life."

"And you can't admit that she's gone. She is," Adam said.

"No, she's not…"

"She is."

"Why do you hate her so much?" Steven asked.

"Because … because she's gone and there's nothing I can do about it."

"But she's not gone."

"She is."

"No, I still see her," Steven said.

"No Steven, you don't. She's gone. Admit that."

"No."

"She's gone."

"No, she's still here. She's still with me."

"No, Steven, she's not. Say it. Please …"

"No."

"Please. Please say it. If you won't I will."

"No." Steven jumped at Adam. He pushed him back. "She's still with me."

"Steven, she's dead. Admit it."

"No."

"Say it. Chris…" Adam spoke with difficulty.

"You fuck."

"Chist … Christin…"

"No." Steven pushed him back once more.
"Christina is gone."
"No. No she's not. Look." Steven pointed behind Adam. "Look behind you."

Adam turned around. Christina stood before him.
"Why do you hate me so much?" she asked.
"No." Adam whispered.
"Why?" Christina asked.
"Because ... because I've done everything to forget you. God, I've tried everything to let you go," Adam said.
"I know," Christina said.
"It's not fair. I've tried but part... "Adam began.
"... of me won't let you go," Steven said.
"How?" Adam asked.
"Why?" Steven asked.
"How could you leave me?" Adam asked.
"I had to," Christina said.
"No, no you didn't," Adam said.
"You didn't..." Steven said.
"... have to go." Adam replied.
"I'm sorry." Christina said.
"Why?" Adam asked.
"I don't know," Christina said.
"Oh God, I miss you Christina," Adam said. "I want to hold you one more time. At least once more. And all I could do was settle for any woman that would fall into my arms. Forgive me. All I could do was hold them or hold on to my anger. That's the only thing that I could do."

"I know," Christina said.

"Oh God." Adam reached slowly for her. "I'd do anything to hold you one more time."

"I know." She embraced him.

"I miss my wife," Adam said.

Christina squeezed him tightly. "I know, Steven. I know but you've got to let me go."

Steven stared on. He watched Adam and Christina vanish before him. The room spun. He saw pictures of Christina, knick knacks from vacations taken together and, various other objects that reminded him of her called out to him while the world twisted round and round. He collapsed.

~ * ~

Steven came to. He found himself on the floor of his apartment's home office. A repeated knock came from outside. He rose, making his way through the living room to the front door where the knocking intensified. He opened the door to find Amy standing outside.

"Are you all right?" she asked.

"Yeah."

"I've been worried sick about you. I must have been knocking on that door for the last half hour."

"I'm sorry."

"I almost called the cops. I didn't know what was wrong."

"I'm fine."

"I love you, Steven." She kissed him.

"I know."

"What is it then?"

"Things are moving so fast for me. I don't know what to do."

"You're so different now. I don't understand you. It's like you're night and day. I can't make you out."

"I know. I'm a strange man."

"No, but it ... it's like there are two totally different sides to you. Some days you're soft and sensitive. Other days, it's like ... I don't know."

Steven nodded.

"Tonight, when you left my house, I didn't know what to think. I don't know what I did to scare you off."

"It's just that ... I'm all mixed up, Amy."

"Why?"

"I never intended for this to happen."

"What do you mean?"

"Us. I'm sorry Amy. I didn't think that things would have turned out the way they have."

"I know it's going to take some time. I understand."

"It's just ... I haven't been able to let go."

"I'm not asking you to. I know you're still very much in love with Christina. I know you don't even want to talk about her at times. I'd just like to give us a try."

"So would I." Steven grabbed her hand. He squeezed it softly.

"You would?" she responded with the same soft grasp.

"Yes."

"Steve." She hugged him.

"Come with me." He led her through the living room to his home office.

"I haven't been in this room before."

"No, this is where I remember her most. In this room. I'd always wait for her here as she got ready. She hated me waiting in the bedroom. It made her feel rushed." Steven paused. He reflected on the last couple of months. "I sit here at times hoping that she'd come back. I never let other people in here."

"Thank you."

He touched Amy's face. He lifted her chin with the tips of his fingers and kissed her as a tear drop ran down his cheek. "Give me time. I need to get myself back together."

"I'll give you all the time I have. Just keep me by your side."

The Meeting

"My name is Jim and I can't stop eating."

Most of the group chuckled at his statement.

"No, it's true," Jim continued. "For years now, I have these fits where I can't stop eating. I'll go on binges that last for hours and hours at a time. Sometimes, even days. No matter what I do, the hunger just won't let me stop. I try and I ... I can't." Jim fell silent as a wave of shame washed over him.

"Thank you for sharing, Jim," said Alex.

Jim nodded to the smattering of applause but remained silent.

The small space that held the nine members of Over Eaters Anonymous seemed more like a cage than a church meeting hall. The members sat on chairs several sizes too small for their large frames. Nearly all the men and women were morbidly obese. Unlike most addicts, these people carried the cross of their affliction in plain sight. Their swollen hands and fat fingers were a testament to their illness. Jim was the only one who was different. He, by comparison, was normal. An average looking man in his forties with no sign of obesity or even a pudge of a weight problem. It was Jim's twelfth meeting. He sat in the back of the room, watching.

Sara stood. "Hi, my name is Sara and I have a food addiction."

"Hi Sara," the group replied.

She smiled. "Most of you know me very well. You all know I've been fighting this issue all my life. Food is the way I cope. I have a bad day, I eat. I have a good day, I want to celebrate so, I eat..."

Jim turned to the two men seated across from him. They were staring. Jim pretended like it didn't bother him. The group's attitude was changing. He could tell fewer and fewer people wanted him at the meetings. At first, they all seemed open and inviting, but now he was met with resentment and distrust. *It's not my fault, my body's different than yours*, he thought. The strange smirk on their faces told Jim that they believed otherwise. He had noticed over the last few meetings how people were turning on him. At first a few people asked what his secret was. If he had gastric bypass surgery or if he was on a special diet. They all hated his reply. No matter what he said, no one would believe the truth. Jim had an addiction to food, and for the most part, his disease was no different than theirs, but his body was different. His metabolism was ten times faster than that of a normal person. It made him the odd man out, with a gift they all wished they could have. He could eat as much as he liked and he would not gain a single pound.

"Thank you for sharing, Sara," Alex replied.

The group clapped in response.

"I thank you all for coming and I'll see you soon," said Alex.

As the members gathered up their belongings, Alex approached Jim.

"Could we talk?" Alex asked.

"Sure," Jim said.

Alex waited until everyone else had left. "Jim, this isn't anything against you. Please don't take it the wrong way, but are there any other meetings you might be able to attend?"

"What?"

"Jim, I only want what's best for everyone. Many people feel you don't need to be here."

"What are you talking about?"

"They don't think you have a problem."

"Why, because I'm not fat? That's bullshit Alex. That's just bull. I come here because I need help and now you're turning me away."

"Let's just look into other options. Face it Jim, you're not like the others here. You're normal. Look, you may have an issue of perception. You may think you eat too much but that may not be the case."

"Do you think I'm crazy Alex? An issue of perception?"

"Jim, let's look into other options. Maybe talk to a counselor and from there see what we can do."

"Thanks. Thanks a lot Alex. I finally find a place where I don't feel so alone and you don't want me here."

"It's not like—"

Jim raised his hand. "No. It is like that. What sort of sponsor are you?"

~ * ~

Jim sat on his kitchen floor. The refrigerator stood naked before him. Within an hour, he had managed to eat a week's worth of groceries. *Maybe an issue of perception. I'll show them.* Jim closed the refrigerator door.

~ * ~

The next day Jim called into work and spent the morning and afternoon at every buffet he could find. At the last Chinese restaurant, he was asked to leave and when he refused, the police were called. As he stormed out of the restaurant he heard the owner say, "In twenty years of owning this place, I've never seen anyone eat like that."

~ * ~

Jim stood in front of the Over Eaters Anonymous group. He held a chain and padlock. "My name is Jim and I can't stop eating." He wrapped the chain around the handles of the double doors and padlocked them shut, sealing off the only exit.

"What are you doing?" Alex asked.

"Shut up Alex," Jim said. "Like I was saying, my name is Jim, and I can't stop eating." He paced back and forth in front of the group. "I was informed that some of you thought this was in my head. That I am not sick or an addict like the rest of you. I guess no one here believed me but, you will."

The group huddled together.

"You see, I do have a problem." Jim tore at his shirt collar. The bones in his neck began to pop as a huge growl escaped from his throat.

The group began to shriek.

"I'm not like the rest of you. I am different in one major way," Jim said. His shoulders widened and as he smiled, his teeth grew. "Since I was a little boy, I've had a hunger that's devoured me." Jim's jaw unhinged and stretched forward.

The group pulled away.

Jim lurched back. "And now, this hunger is going to devour you."

Found Note

The boys of the village do not cry. Tears are forbidden. If they are seen crying, they are banished. They are given a small sack of food packed in a hemp-woven blanket. The blankets were once used to wrap the boys when they were born. That is all they can take with them if they are found crying.

The boys of the village are not allowed to question the men who beat their mothers. They are not allowed to stand up to the men when they are old enough. If they do, the boys of the village are banished.

The boys of the village cannot ask the women of the village why they love the men who hurt them. The boys cannot feel ashamed when they walk through the village holding their mothers' hands, while their mothers weep bloodstained tears.

The boys of the village do not play. They sit and stare into the sunset when day disappears. Many wonder if any of the banished ones ever survive.

The boys of the village cannot question the girls who love the men who hit them. The boys cannot defend the girls they love. If they do, they are banished. The sack of food bound in the hemp-woven blankets will not give them enough nourishment to venture past the wasteland. The boys starve shortly afterward.

The boys of the village cannot feel. The boys of the village cannot love. They must become the men of the village.

The boys of the village cannot tell others about the rules of the village. They cannot write about the village. They are forbidden to do so.

I have lived in the village my entire life. I am scared. I am hungry. The food in my hemp sack is gone. I rest and look into the sunset. I remind myself that the boys of the village cannot cry. The boys of the village cannot...

Occupation

"I'm just a thief," Danny said. He winked at the girl sitting across from him at the bar.

"Really?" she replied with a smile.

"Yeah." He knew he was in. Girls like this always liked bad boys and considering they were on the strip in Vegas, she most likely wanted the baddest.

"How long have you been in that sort of work?" she asked.

"About seven years or so." He eyed her up and down. She couldn't have been older than 24. Her long tanned legs made him guess that she was a career college student living off daddy's money.

"Do you like it?" she asked.

"Well, I like being my own boss but the benefits suck."

She laughed and placed her hand on his forearm. "Are you really a thief?"

"Yeah. You don't believe me?" he asked.

"I don't know. I have my doubts."

"Do you?" He motioned to the bartender that he needed another round of drinks and then faced the girl once more. "What sort of doubts?"

"Well, if you were a thief, why would you tell anyone?"

"Good question. Maybe I trust you," he said with a smile. "And maybe I don't work in Vegas."

"Oh, so that means you don't trust me."

"Can't help it. Comes with the territory."

"Then how can I trust you? Maybe this is all a lie to get me interested. Maybe you're a boring accountant who goes home to a wife and three kids and you're in sin city for a convention."

"I can prove it to you."

"How?"

He inched closer and whispered, "We can break into a place tonight. You and me."

"What sort of girl do you take me for?" she asked playfully.

"The kind that wants a little adventure."

"And what sort of troublesome adventure are you thinking about?"

"A little B and E. It's sort of my specialty."

"Really?"

He nodded.

"And where shall we break into?" she asked.

"I'll leave that little challenge up to you but we have to do it as a bet."

"Okay, what's the wager?" she asked.

"You pick the spot and if I can get us into it, well … we'll just see how the rest of the evening progresses.

"Fine," she said.

"But it has to be reasonable. Don't ask me to break into a vault somewhere. Let's do a place of residence, hotel room, apartment. Something like that. If I think I can do it, I'll take the challenge."

"And if you can't?"

"I'll ask for another one."

"Okay, how about this." She placed her hand on his thigh and whispered, "Break into a suite at the Wynn."

"Meet me in the lobby in 30 minutes."

~ * ~

Danny waved at the girl as she waited near the service desk in the Wynn's lobby. She waved back and then raced over to him.

"So, are we all set?" she asked.

"Almost, I need you to help me," he told her. "Upstairs, we need to find a maid. I need you to talk to her until I give you the sign."

"What's the sign?"

"How about I just wave you over?"

"Okay."

"Follow me." He led her to the elevator and in a few minutes they found an attendant pushing a cart. The girl approached the maid while Danny slid behind her. In the exchange he stole the maid's key card without her knowing. He waved when he got to the end of the hall.

The girl raced over to him when the attendant turned the corner.

"So?" she asked.

What's the easiest way to break into a place?" he asked.

"I don't know."

He lifted the key card up for her to see. "Use a key."

She laughed.

"Come on." They ran to the elevator and pressed the button for the top floor.

"There's only two different rooms we can sneak into," he said. "I called earlier and asked the front desk what suites were available and I got her to tell me which ones were on hold. We don't want any surprise visits from guests."

"I can't believe we're doing this," she said.

"Exciting, right?"

"Oh yes." She leaned into him.

"One more thing."

"What is it?" she asked.

"We can't steal anything. We'll be breaking in but can't do anything that could raise suspicions when we leave. If nothing's missing, no one will know or care."

~ * ~

The girl rested her head on Danny's chest. The moonlight made her naked skin glow. She tilted her head and looked up at him.

"That was nice," she said.

"Yeah, it was."

"So, you really are a thief."

"I told you."

"A girl could get used to something like this. Are you looking for a partner in crime?"

He smiled. "I wish, but no. I don't think you'd like the ugly part of the job."

"Tell me about it."

"Well, you have to watch people. Figure them out. Their schedules, their routines, if they're likely to have some sort of home protection. Stuff like that. And sometimes you find someone who you can't understand."

"What do you mean?"

"There's this house I hit about a month ago. The owner seemed like a quiet guy, worked a regular nine to five and had some really nice things. I made a decent amount of money from the job. I even grabbed a set of keys in the off chance that he doesn't change out the locks and that whatever security system he puts in won't be hard to bypass."

Okay?"

"Well, here's the thing I'm having trouble with. It doesn't seem like he cared. He hasn't done anything that I can see to protect the house and he's even restocked it with new electronics. I mean, he'll leave the empty boxes of whatever he's purchased out in plain sight. Most of the time he's leaving the stuff in the trash for curbside pick-up but he's not covering any of it up. I can tell exactly what he has. I wonder how someone could be so stupid."

"Maybe he thinks you're not coming back."

"That's the thing I don't understand. Most people usually go overboard with security when their homes get broken into. This guy doesn't care. He's almost announcing to the world, I got some new shit. Come take it."

"Are you?" Her eyes lit up with the question.

"What?"

"Are you going to take it?"

"As soon as I return home."

~ * ~

Danny sat in his van patiently waiting for the house to be empty. He glanced through his binoculars every now and then to be sure he didn't miss anything. He looked at his watch. It was 8:20 am. In another ten minutes the owner should leave and he would have enough time to do what he needed to do.

Danny fantasized about the girl in Vegas. He never asked for her name. He didn't want to know anything about her that could make her more than just a fling but he did miss her. She gave him her number the morning after. Danny tossed it out the moment she left. He couldn't have ties to the world. He never wanted anyone around that might expose him as a thief and he never wanted to hurt anyone who could love him if he got caught.

Danny looked up and noticed the owner pulling away in his Ford Explorer. For a moment, Danny envied him. A guy like that could call the girl the next morning. He could ask for her name. Maybe even have a comfortable life with her.

Danny was beginning to hate the guy. He no longer felt remotely sorry about robbing him a second time.

Danny waited until the Explorer turned out of sight before getting out of the van. He placed a magnetic sign on the door that read Smith Electrical and parked the van in the driveway.

He grabbed some large duffle bags and walked to the front of the house. The house appeared no different than the first time he broke in a month ago. There were no security cameras on the outside or anything that looked like an alarm system on the inside.

Danny fished out the key from his pocket. He slid it into the lock and turned the key.

The door opened.

"So simple," he said to himself. He thought of the suite at the Wynn. *What's the easiest way to break into a place? Use a key.*

Danny reached into his pocket and pulled out a pair of latex gloves. He opened the first duffel bag and raced into the bedroom. He doubted the owner had replaced any of the jewelry he lost but he checked just the same.

A small box lay on the bedroom dresser. Danny opened it and found a Rolex inside. "This must be the dumbest person I've ever robbed," he said. He picked up the watch.

A door slammed behind him.

Danny spun around.

The bedroom door was closed.

He ran to the door, turned the knob and yanked with all his might.

Nothing happened.

He pulled and pulled and then decided to try slamming his shoulder into the door. It didn't budge. He realized the door, hinges and frame were all metal and painted over with white paint.

"What the hell is going on?" he asked.

Danny ran to the window. He removed a flashlight from his pocket and crashed the butt of the light against the glass.

The window didn't buckle. It seemed to be made of some shatter resistant plexiglass.

Danny thrashed around the room, looking for a way out.

He spotted a large wall clock that rested over the bed. It wasn't there the first time he broke into the house. There was something different about the clock.

Danny removed it from the wall. Hidden behind the clock was a small camera. He was being watched. The owner had set the room up like a prison cell and now, Danny was trapped.

A hiss came from the camera. Danny examined the device. Underneath the camera was a second opening.

The hiss came again. This time, a faint mist of smoke came from the camera's opening.

Danny jumped back.

The smoke increased until a cloud filled the room.

Danny felt weak. He dropped to the floor to avoid the smoke.

"Get me out of here!" he yelled.

The smoke thickened.

"Help, help me..." As the words escaped his lips, the room started to spin and Danny passed out.

~ * ~

Danny awoke strapped to a metal table. His hands and legs were bound to each corner and his head and torso were held down by leather straps. He struggled to move, but couldn't. He couldn't even turn his head.

"What is this?" he demanded.

Danny tried to examine what he could of the room. It seemed to be a windowless space with white walls. Two bright lights glared into his face.

"Get me out of here," Danny insisted.

A figure emerged from the corner.

"Help. Help me," Danny said.

The figure stood in front of Danny. It was the man who owned the house. He wore a green surgeon's outfit covered by a large plastic apron.

"What's going on?" Danny asked.

"You like to steal from people, don't you?" asked the man.

"Oh God. Please mister," Danny pleaded.

"Don't you?"

"Oh God, what are you going to do?" Danny asked.

"Answer the question."

"Yes. Yes, I do. Please let me go."

"Can't do that."

"Oh God, mister. Please. Whatever you want, I'll let you have it. I'll get you all your stuff back. Please. I'm sorry."

The man shook his head.

"Please. Please mister. I'm just a thief. That's all. That's all I am. I'm sorry. I'm just a thief."

The man pulled out a knife and smiled at Danny. "And I'm just a butcher."

666

"So, the mark of the beast?" asked Jason.

The tall man nodded, "Yes."

Jason looked down at his customer's drawing. It was an intricate combination of tiny tribal symbols that, from a distance, resembled three sixes.

"And that's exactly how you want the tattoo to look?" asked Jason.

"Exactly like that," said the stranger.

Jason grabbed the paper and walked around the booth. He entered his cluttered office in the corner of his tattoo parlor while the man waited on the opposite side of the glass counter. "I hate being alone whenever one of these Armageddon freaks come in," Jason whispered half to himself, half as a prayer.

Armageddon freaks were a mixture of weirdos and nuts and New Age anarchists who believed that Doomsday was drawing near. Never-ending news feeds via web, cell phone, and other immediate access media pumped war, climate change and other world catastrophes into the collective consciousness. A new subculture, drowned in despair, had emerged—individuals who felt the Antichrist was coming.

Most of the people Jason labeled as Armageddon freaks liked to wear the mark of the beast as a symbol of their anti-establishment beliefs. Many wore tee-shirts, pins, or jewelry with the three sixes. Some fanatics wanted tattoos.

Jason copied the man's drawing and prepared it to be transferred onto his skin. He returned to the stranger.

"Here, have a seat." Jason pointed to the chair where he inked his clients.

The man sat down.

"Where do you want it?" asked Jason.

"Right shoulder."

The man took off his shirt. Jason put on a pair of latex gloves and prepped the area for ink.

"You don't believe, do you?" asked the man.

"What?" Jason asked, not sure if he really wanted to hear the question again.

"You don't believe that he's coming, do you?"

"It's not my business to believe. It's my business to give my clients the best artwork I can. That's all," Jason replied.

"What if I tell you that it's important? That it's the only way I'll be able to have the tattoo done?"

"Do you want this thing or don't you?" Jason asked.

"I do but I need to have it done by a fellow follower," said the man.

"If you're telling me I have to believe the Devil is coming to end the world, to bring about our destruction, to bring Armageddon, before I can give you this tat, sure. I believe it, man. The customer is always right."

The man shook his head. "No, it's what has to be for it to be done."

"Should I stop?" asked Jason. "If you don't want me as your artist, I'll give you a list of other parlors in the area."

"No, I want you to do it."

Jason prepped the needles and tattoo gun. He grabbed the man's arm and pressed the gun to his shoulder.

The needles jabbed at the man's skin but wouldn't pierce it.

"What the hell?" Jason asked. He pushed the gun hard against the man's flesh.

The needles broke leaving the man's skin untouched.

The stranger turned toward Jason. "You can't mark the beast, unless you believe in the beast," he said with a big smile.

Jason's heart skipped a beat when he saw the man's forked tongue.

Journal Found in Woods

11-10-11

I'm scared. My four friends and I have been lost in the mountains for an entire day. We were hit by several unexpected storms and lost our bearings. We cannot find our way back.

I was bitten two hours ago. As dusk fell, while I was collecting wood for our campfire, an animal attacked me. I could not see what it was. I could only tell that it was large and wanted to kill me.

The creature grabbed me and went for my throat. I hunched my shoulders. It missed my neck, and bit my right shoulder.

Tim fired his shotgun, barely hitting the animal, and it got away.

I'm worried. Tim and Peter bandaged my wound. They think I need medical help. More snow is coming tonight and we won't be able to leave until daybreak. I don't know how much time I have.

~ * ~

11-11-11

We found a stream and plan to follow it down. There may be others who have made camp further down the mountain.

I've developed a fever. I need help.

My friends say I'm making strange noises. I don't know what they mean. I just want to go home.

~ * ~

11-12-11

Thirsty. So thirsty. I drink and drink and can't satisfy the thirst.

The fever has gotten worse. I'm burning up. My friends can't look into my eyes. They say my eyes look weird and the noises I make are getting worse. I also passed out today. I'll be dead soon.

~ * ~

11-13-11

The thirst. I drink and drink but nothing. I eat snow for the thirst and to help ease the fever. Still nothing. My friends are scared of me. They tell me I say strange things, that I make even weirder noises, especially at night.

I ... I keep passing out. Peter thinks the bite has given me something. Rabies or an infection of some sort. He believes that's why I'm so thirsty. The infection is affecting my pancreas. He doesn't know what it is or what it could be. I've never seen him this terrified in all my life.

~ * ~

11-14-11

I'm so damn thirsty. It hurts. My throat's raw. I can't stand it. The thirst doesn't let me think straight.

We've made it further down the stream. It's more progress than we dared hope for. My friends think we might actually make it but they're still terrified of me.

I heard Lisa whispering to Tim and Peter that I need to be watched constantly. Jamie agreed. My behavior scares them.

I keep passing out.

~ * ~

11-15-11

Blood. So much blood. When I awoke this morning I was covered in blood. My friends have vanished. I don't know what's happened. I can't find a trace of them. Only blood. It's everywhere. The crimson glows against the white snow. My friends are missing.

The only good thing is I'm no longer thirsty.

The Writers' Group

They sat at a round, mahogany table with a small, skin-bound book resting in the center. They stared at the pale pages held in place by near seamless stitching. Each held a pad in one hand, a pen in the other. Each took a turn shaping the story. Each added what was needed and then subtracted what was not. Five writers, five hands twitching at pens that formed a story.

"I don't like it," said the first. "It's not enough. How could he do all those things by then? It's just not possible."

"I agree," said the second writer. "That much heartache is going to break him."

"What about all the times he won't feel up to it? All the times he'll feel broken, both body and soul?" asked the third.

"You'll need faith," said the fourth. "It can happen."

"I want to write the ending," said the fifth.

Each spoke in turn, from the first to the last, as the writers created the plot and built the character.

"I don't see it happening like you see it. Not at all," said the first to the fourth.

The second turned and agreed, "Too much drama. It's not going to happen."

The third nodded. "True."

"You have to give him a chance. All of you," said the fourth. "Lay off and give him a chance."

"The ending," demanded the fifth.

The rest ignored him.

"Not enough—"

"Too much—"

"The pain—"

"Give him a chance."

"The ending."

The circle of voices grew louder.

"He'll need more—"

"His heart will—"

"Bedridden most of his—"

"He has heart, it will—"

"It needs to—"

"There won't be—"

"He'll suffer too—"

"The days and nights—"

"Give him a chance."

"It needs—"

The fourth writer rose and slammed his fist down on the table.

The group was silent.

The skin-bound book in the center of the table shifted and shook.

All eyes focused as it bumped and twitched. Slowly, from beneath its hard cover, a pair of small, pale legs grew. Then, a pair of arms. Finally a head emerged from the pages. The book became a newborn. The baby opened its mouth. Its cry shattered the silence.

The fourth writer spoke, "You have to give him a chance."

One by one they tore pages from their pads and fed the child their influences.

Time was first. On his pages he gave the child the number of days he would have to live his life.

Then came Sorrow. He gave the child the pain that would shape him.

Illness followed with the afflictions that would limit him.

The fourth writer, Destiny, rose. "Give him a chance. That is all I want."

Death, the fifth writer, tore a page from his book and gave it to the newborn. "I don't know why everyone is so distraught. It's only life."

The Last Song

"So, tomorrow's the big night." Eric said. He raised his beer bottle to toast.

James shook his head as if coming out of a dream. "What?"

"Tomorrow, big night. Last performance of the year," Eric said. "You must be excited."

James smiled but it was a stage smile. Something you learned to do while on the road or on stage to give the illusion of a smile. To most people, it would look real. It would appear genuine but to Eric—he knew better.

"What's wrong?" Eric asked.

"Nothing." James turned on his bar stool. Aside from the half sleeping bartender at the corner of the room, Eric and James were alone.

"James, I've been on the road with you this whole year. You can't fool me. Something's wrong," Eric said.

"Just thinking about the last song."

"That's your hit, man. Everyone loves that song."

James nodded. Eric was his guitar player and the one guy in the group who James considered a friend.

"You worried about that song?" Eric asked.

"Eric, can I talk to you?"

"Sure, man. You know me."

"No, I mean, really talk to you?"

"Yeah. What's up?" Eric asked.

"About a year ago, I was a nobody," James said.

"What are you talking about?"

"Before the album. Before the gigs, the tour, everything like that, I was a normal guy with nothing special or even worthwhile in my life."

"We've all felt like that," Eric said. "When you're not playing or your music's not going anywhere. It sucks. You feel like a nobody."

"Eric, it's not that." James shook his head. "I literally was a nobody. I wasn't a musician. I couldn't read music, write music. Hell, I couldn't even sing Happy Birthday without someone at the party asking me to stop."

"Get out of here," Eric said.

"I'm serious. Listen, a year ago I couldn't do any of this stuff." James paused and took a long deep breath. "Last year, I went through a breakup. A really bad breakup. I decided to take a little vacation and go as far away from everything I knew for at least a few months. I grabbed all I could stuff into a bag, made a few calls, jumped into my car and drove. I wanted to go as far as I could and just see the States for once. I traveled all over. Constantly heading west when I could, and north when I couldn't. I stayed with friends all over the U.S. I thought the trip would do me some good. That I'd see the world differently. That maybe it might help me see my own life differently. I don't know. I just wanted to change and get out of the hell I was in. The problem was, the more I traveled, the more my past haunted me."

Eric nodded.

"The trip ended with me passed out at a friend's apartment in Seattle. The radiator in my car had died and I was stuck there for at least a week before I could do anything. So, I got bored. Each night I'd find another place to go, another nightclub to check out and I really started to like Seattle's music scene. One night I went to check out a brother and sister act at the Edgewater Hotel."

Eric smiled. "I know the Edgewater and Seattle all too well."

"Yeah, it seemed like the hotel's history was entwined with music itself. Anyway, I sat in the hotel's restaurant and listened to these two musicians all night. I was beyond captivated. They performed their own songs and they did covers. It was amazing. For the first time in a long while I forgot about the breakup. Their music was magic. Then, the brother sang a song called *Love is Blind*. The song broke me in half. I sat in the back of the room with tears in my eyes. The lyrics cried out to every emotion I ever felt about my ex, Amy. The hopes I ever had for us. The dreams I lost. The wishes and desires I secretly carried deep within me. I traveled thousands of miles away from home to escape. Instead, I discovered the truth that I hid from myself. I discovered it through this song. Even though I knew I could never get back with Amy. Even though I knew it was over, deep down, that's what I wanted. I wanted her back. This song, this performer made me aware of it. He was able to put into words everything that I felt." James took a sip of his rum and Coke. "At that moment

I wished I could do what this performer could. I'd give anything to write out exactly what my heart felt. I'd give anything to do that. At least once."

Eric smiled and said, "Then you started writing music? Man, that's amazing."

James shook his head. "Not exactly. That night, I stayed in the restaurant until it closed. I couldn't move. I had such an emotional discharge, I felt paralyzed. I tried to work through the whole trip, the break up, where I was with everything. I needed answers. I sat there for hours. At the end of the night, when the restaurant closed and I was politely asked to leave, a man approached me in the hotel lobby. He wore this dark black suit. I mean, the fabric was so dark it seemed stitched together from the strands of nightmares. Well, he asked me about the show. I told him I've never been moved like that before. He asked me if I ever thought about making music. I told him how I was terrible at it and that I couldn't carry a single note. He laughed and said he could change all that. I didn't know what he was getting at. He said he had a way to make me not only sing, but become a great performer. He asked if I was interested. I was. I never felt so alive and at the same time, so destroyed as I did listening to that song. I would have loved to have been able to affect people the same way." James turned to Eric. "I promised this man. Things."

"What do you mean?" Eric asked.

"I promised him my life, Eric. My life and my soul."

"Come on, you're pulling my leg," Eric said.

"No. I'm not. I promised this man my soul and my life if he could give me that power. That night I went home and wrote my first song. In the days that followed, I kept writing. Within a week, I had an album. I bought a keyboard and I could play anything. The friend I was staying with in Seattle heard me playing and introduced me to some musicians. And the rest, as they say, is history."

"Are you serious?" Eric asked.

"I'm sitting here beside you because of a promise I made. After tomorrow's performance, I'm going to vanish and no one will see me again."

"Stop pulling my leg." Eric laughed. "You got me, man. You got me." Eric raised his beer. "Here's to a great song writer and story teller."

James raised his glass as well and smiled.

"That was a good one," Eric said as he made his way to the hotel lobby. "I'm going to go upstairs and get some rest. I can't wait to tell the guys we're touring with a guy who sold his soul."

"Eric, do me a favor," James said.

Eric turned around.

"Keep this joke between us," James said.

~ * ~

The moments before you hit the stage, there's a feeling of dread, excitement, fear, hope, and every other emotion you can imagine that rushes through you. It's the second before the first drop of a rollercoaster or the shock of jumping out of an airplane. It can get you hooked the moment the adrenaline courses through your veins.

James stood behind the curtains, peering out at the crowd. The rise and fall of his heart rate was intoxicating. He waited for the excitement to fill his body with energy. But tonight, along with the usual charge, came something else. A sadness. It was his last night on stage and his last night alive. He wondered if Amy would be in the crowd tonight. He wondered if she received the tickets and invitation and if she planned on showing up.

He wondered if Eric believed him. He wondered how it would happen. Would he just disappear? Would it be painful?

The stage lights came on. James found the strength to focus. His thoughts about fulfilling his part of the promise didn't matter. He was expected to perform and as they say, the show must go on.

~ * ~

James covered the play list front to back and threw in several covers he hadn't practiced with the rest of the band. They managed to keep up without a problem. He decided to cover the song, *Love is Blind*. He felt it fitting and wanted to perform the song that made him sell his soul. During one point in the song, the stage lights twisted and lit up part of the crowd. Seated center stage, front row, was Amy. It was the first time James noticed her. The stage lights were too bright, and he had a habit of concentrating on his performance and not the crowd. But tonight, he could see Amy. She had received the tickets. She made it to the show.

James smiled.

The lights moved once more and James noticed a familiar face seated two rows behind Amy. It was the man he met a year ago at the Edgewater Hotel. The man with the dark suit. The nightmares were about to begin.

James finished the last lyrics of *Love is Blind* and started into, *The Last Song*. The lights dimmed and everyone in the audience was silent.

The lyrics poured from James as easily as ever. *"This is the last song that you'll have to hear. These are my last words, our love was dear."*

Eric followed with his acoustic guitar. The cords hung sweetly in the air.

"I drove one day to find myself but instead I found you," sang James. *"I drove to hell and back to forget but found there was nothing I could do. Instead of finding myself, I found you."*

As James finished the last lyrics, tears rolled down his face.

Eric's finger's plucked at the last notes of the song. As the last strings stopped vibrating, the crowd erupted with applause.

James wiped the tears from his face and smiled.

The audience stood.

Amy, was crying. The man in the dark suit behind her smiled.

James and the rest of the band took their bows and walked off stage.

Eric clapped James on the shoulder and said, "Great show."

"Yeah, great show," James replied.

~ * ~

James entered his dressing room. The man in the dark suit was waiting inside.

"Congratulations," said the man.

"Thank you," James said.

"Well, we had a deal. You got your part of it, now we have to go."

"I know. I made a deal with the devil and—"

"Let's not start calling each other names. Besides, I don't like being called the devil. You made a deal with a stranger and you seemed like the type of guy who would honor his deals."

James nodded.

"I have to ask you one thing," the stranger said. "Was it worth the price?"

James thought for a moment. "I lost my soul the moment I fell in love with Amy. I realized that the night I met you. If it took selling my soul to finally find a way of telling her how I felt, so be it."

"No regrets?" asked the man.

"No. Not after tonight."

The man smiled. "Well, there's one little problem."

"What is it?" James asked.

"Like you said, you lost your soul when you met Amy. You can't barter with something you don't have."

"What do you mean?"

"I can't take your soul. In fact, I made a mistake even creating our little contract. It seems dealing with a man who would trade his soul to tell the women he loves that he still cares in front of the world, isn't such a good trade off. Besides, I had a bet with the devil myself. I bet I could find a man that would be willing to go to hell and back for love."

"Wait, you're not the—"

"Devil?" the stranger smiled. "No. I never said I was."

"Then what are you?" James asked.

"Just a guy helping a lost soul find its way back home."

A knock came from the door.

James turned toward the door and then turned back. The stranger was gone.

The knock came again.

James opened the door and found Amy waiting outside.

A Father's Warning

"Don't walk in the woods east of the river," my father warned. "Don't walk through those woods, no matter what the reason," he'd warn me and my brothers. "Everywhere else is fine and safe but the woods east of the river are not allowed."

We'd ask and even beg for one reason. Just to know why those woods were off limits. We kept bothering him until finally one night he answered.

"There are monsters and ghosts and demons back there." Never once did my father smile or give us reason to believe it was a joke.

Time passed and, as good children, we listened. We never set foot in the woods east of the river.

Seasons came and went and good children turned into good men who moved away to start families of their own. And as time pressed on, good men grew old and fathers grew older until the day came that our father died.

We returned home to say good-bye. We kissed our father on the forehead one last time and buried him in the family plot a few miles from the river.

That day, I walked through the fields my father kept and touched the crops my father grew. I made my way to the river, and before long, I found myself at the edge of the forbidden woods.

I lost my father that day, and maybe it made me lose my way, but I found myself walking into the woods east of the river. I wanted to find the monsters and ghosts and demons that lay deep within. I walked and walked until night took over day. I waited for the monsters, the ghosts, and the demons. I waited and waited until I heard a sound come from behind me. I turned to find my father waiting for me.

"Why did you come here?" he asked.

"I had to know," I said. "I had to know about the monsters and demons."

"Did you not believe me?"

"I don't know."

"Did I ever lie to you?"

"No."

"Well then look." He clapped his hands together. From the darkness emerged werewolves and beasts. Trees shook and from under their roots sprouted horned demons and red devils.

"Do you believe me now?" he asked.

"Yes. Yes I do," I cried and cried and asked him to forgive me.

The monsters crept closer to me.

"I'm sorry," I said. "Please forgive me."

He moved through the creatures and took my hand, kissed my forehead and said, "I know you were always a curious child. A child who didn't believe in monsters but I only wanted to protect you."

"I'm sorry."

"I know. I know but it's time to leave this place."

My father took my hand and led me out of the woods east of the river.

Getting Personal

'An unforgettable smile with an unforgivable longing.' That's what the singles' ad read. Charlie reread the ad he'd cut out of the personals section of the paper. 'SWF in search of that special someone. Alone in the dark, longing for company.'

Charlie ordered another drink while he looked over the small piece of newsprint. The bartender slid over a scotch and Coke. Charlie sipped it.

"It's getting late," said the bartender. "We're closing in a little while."

Charlie put a fifty dollar bill down on the counter. "She'll be here."

The bartender picked up the bill and took a deep breath. "I don't know how to say this but it's been two hours. I'm not saying she stood you up on purpose but..."

"You don't think she's going to be here because it's me." Charlie looked at his reflection in the mirror behind the bar. His short, chubby image stared back at him through a pair of out-dated eye glasses. "Because no woman would be caught dead with a guy like me."

"Charlie, you tell me she's a six foot tall brunette with looks that could give a man a heart attack. She put an ad in the paper to find love. Why would a woman like that need to do such a thing? Why would a woman like that need to search for romance?"

Charlie straightened up on the bar stool. "Because she's tired of the guys she's been meeting. Because she scares guys off with her looks."

"And you know this, how?"

"That's what she told me when we spoke on the phone."

"But you've never seen her?"

"No…"

The bartender stood back. He ran his fingers through his hair and grabbed a beer for himself. "You meet this girl through the paper. She may not be what she's pretending to be. Look, I once agreed to be set up with a friend of a friend. I spoke to this girl on the phone for hours. She told me she was a knockout. That she had a porn star's body, an angel's face, and that she couldn't find dates because her job didn't give her enough time to get out and meet people. Charlie, I raced through the city and drove 60 miles to meet this girl. When I got there, I discovered a woman who had Ron Jeremy's body, had a devil's face, and the real reason she couldn't find any dates was you had to be legally blind to find her attractive."

Charlie shook his head. "It's not like that. I believe her. I ... I have to."

"What do you mean?"

"Look at me. Just look. What prospects do I have? I haven't had a real date in over three years and I haven't had a girlfriend since college. This woman's given me a chance. I have to believe it's real. I told her what to expect. I told her what she's getting into and she still wants to meet me. Besides, I connected with her. I don't know what it is. There's something in her voice, her charm, that doesn't let me pull away."

"Okay. There's no one here. I still have a lot of work to do before I can leave tonight. You're more than welcome to stay here while I close up but in another half hour, if she's not here, I'm going to have to lock up and..."

The door opened. A brunette stepped in from the dark. Both men stopped in their tracks. The brunette's features sparkled under the soft glow of neon, and when she moved, she floated.

"Charlie?" she asked.

"Yes?" Charlie replied, shocked, stunned and surprised.

"I'm sorry I'm late. I overslept."

"No, no it's okay."

She turned toward the bartender, "I'm Valarie, by the way."

He shook her hand.

"I see you're closing up, I'm sorry if I've kept you here longer than you expected," she said.

"No, it's fine," the bartender replied. He leaned closer to Charlie. "Oh, and what we were talking about, forget everything I mentioned."

"There's a place not too far from here that's still open. We could talk if you're not too upset with me," she said.

"Okay." Charlie waved to the bartender and left the bar with the woman of his dreams.

~ * ~

Charlie and Valarie sat on a park bench hidden from the world under the blanket of night. The moon made her white skin sparkle, and the more Charlie talked to Valarie, the more beautiful she became.

"I've really wanted to meet you," he said. "I didn't know what to expect but it felt so right."

"Has it?" she asked.

"Yes, why? Do you feel differently?"

"No, Charlie. I don't." She waved away a strand of hair that fell to her cheek. The gesture was small but the grace in the movement, followed by the softness in her blue eyes, broke Charlie.

"Why are we here?" he asked.

"To talk."

"No, why are you here with me? Out of all the guys in the world, why are you with a short guy who can't see a foot in front of his face if he didn't have glasses? Is this a joke?"

"No. It's not. I told you—"

"That you scare guys off," he interrupted. "Well, don't I scare you? Don't you think I'm too ordinary? Too boring?"

"Do you believe in love?" she asked.

"I don't know."

"Charlie, look at me. Do you believe in love?"

He stared into her eyes. Her pupils dilated and then the iris faded from a baby blue to a light green then back to blue again. Charlie was drawn in. He felt like a boy again—looking into the ocean for the first time. He was at a loss for words.

"I believe you do," she said. "You answered a complete stranger's ad not caring what or who you'd meet. You waited at that bar for me for over two hours and refused to leave until I arrived. You believe in love. That's why I'm here. I have a secret to tell you." She leaned in to him. "I'm different and that's what scares everyone away."

She smiled and for the first time, Charlie could see her canines were twice as long as a normal person's. Her eyes changed colors again and Charlie knew just how different she was.

"You see now, why I needed to meet you like this?" she asked.

"Yes."

She held his hand. "I also believe in love. Stay. Stay here with me and let's forget who and what we are and just concentrate on what we believe."

Charlie stared back into her eyes. He leaned in closer to her lips. "Valarie, you do have an unforgettable smile."

Under an elm tree, covered by night, two strangers found love because they believed in it.

The Fisherman

My wife and I first encountered the island by chance. It was on our first vacation together, twenty-five years ago. I was working full-time as an intern at Massachusetts General Hospital. Fulltime meant every waking hour. Jamie had come to terms with the isolation she found being a doctor's wife. I know we survived our first year of marriage because of Jamie's patience and understanding. It was her idea to go away for two weeks. A chance to reconnect. She wanted Hawaii. I wanted something less touristy but would have settled for anything that kept us happy and sunburned on a beach rather than bitter and angry in divorce court. To juggle a job as demanding as mine and a love as passionate as Jamie's was difficult. I never wanted to be forced to choose between the two.

We both agreed that a less populated spot would be ideal. Our travel agent worked out the details and we ended up on a small stretch of land known as Otium Island. Only a few hundred people lived on the island back then. On our return twenty-five years later we discovered little had changed since our first visit.

Our tiny two-bedroom beach house was littered with large boxes and furniture that needed to be unpacked and arranged. I took a break from settling in to admire the ocean from the outside deck. The sea was beautiful. Especially at night. The island waters sparkled unlike any other place I have ever visited. The shoreline seemed speckled with gold and the sand littered with diamonds. You could see the moon and the stars as easily in the reflection of the soft lapping waves as you could in the sky above.

We had one neighbor who lived east of us, a fisherman. The only fisherman on the island. He lived in a shack that made our two bedroom house seem like a palace.

I glanced toward his home. A small light burned from within. The fisherman was still up.

A spark of lightning lit up the horizon several miles out over the ocean. The clap of thunder rolled over the waves and when it finally reached the island, it was barely a whisper.

The light in the fisherman's house died. A second later, an old man emerged from the small shack. A large net was folded and draped over his left shoulder. In his right hand was a large harpoon. He made his way to an overturned wooden boat resting on the beach.

It was a strange time to go fishing.

"Thomas," Jamie called.

I left the fisherman to the ocean and tended to my wife.

Jamie was in bed. A single sheet covered her.

"How do you feel?" I asked.

"Well. I'd like to take a bath."

"Do you want me to help you—"

"No. I actually feel strong enough but could you stay near me. Just in case."

I forced a smile and nodded.

"Thank you."

I brushed her cheek with my hand and kissed her. Time is never kind to any of us but to me, Jamie was still as beautiful as ever. Somehow, even more than when we first met.

I walked her to the bathroom, holding her arm. The handrails installed over the bathtub caught my eye and made me feel lost for a second.

They gave her a year, at the most. Less than a year if the treatments and the surgery didn't help.

It was best not to think about Jamie's illness. Instead, I wondered how the fisherman was doing in the storm just off the island.

~ * ~

"Thomas, Thomas, wake up." Jamie shook me from my dreams.

"What? What's wrong?"

Jamie stood over me, awake and alive as ever. "I made breakfast."

"You ... you made breakfast?"

Jamie smiled. She held my hand and walked me to the kitchen. She sat me down at the table. I rubbed the sleep from my eyes and was amazed to find a full spread of food laid out before me; everything from pancakes, to cut fruit.

"Jamie, you shouldn't have."

She kissed my forehead and then sat across from me.

I wanted to tell her not to exert herself. I wanted to say that it's best to let me do all the work. That it would be better for her. I wanted to, but couldn't. Something had awoken within her. A spark that I hadn't seen in a while. Maybe it was the memory of this place. Maybe it was the thought of those first few days we spent here together so many years ago. I may have been too concerned with her illness, and how things might be in another year to remember our first visit, but she was dealing with things differently.

I looked down at the plate in front of me. "I don't know where to start."

I cut a small bite size piece from the stack of pancakes with the side of my fork. I brought the piece to my mouth. I chewed slowly, scared that I may lose my appetite and ruin Jamie's mood. I could never hide my thoughts and feelings from her. If anything bad crossed my mind, Jamie knew.

I glanced up at her. She had eaten a good portion of what was on her plate.

"We have an appointment today at two," she said.

"I know. We'll have to leave here around noon to catch the ferry at one."

"Maybe we can leave here earlier."

"Why?" I asked.

"I'd like to see a few of the places on the island. See if anything's changed."

"Are you sure you'll be fine?" I brought another bite up to my lips.

"Yes."

I nodded and chewed. I didn't know how much more strength she would have. I hoped that it would last until we left the island and made it to the hospital. I knew the treatments would have their effect on her. I knew she'd definitely be tired by then. I'd have to conserve my energy to help her and to finish unpacking.

I remembered the boxes, the stack of items still left to sort out. The pile of clothes, books, and other knick-knacks that needed to be put away. I glanced back at the living room.

Everything was gone.

"What happened to the boxes in the living room?" I asked.

"Oh, I put that stuff away while you were asleep."

~ * ~

Jamie and I walked through the small market place. She held my hand. Every once and a while she would give my fingers a squeeze and occasionally she'd surprise me with a smile.

I was still upset over the amount of work Jamie had done at the beach house. The doctors were clear. She needs to rest, but Jamie had always been a little stubborn. I tried to forget about it as we strolled through the shops on the island.

Little had changed on Otium Island. It was as if this place had been preserved through a mix of the island air and the salted sea. My memories of island life back then were no different than my moments now. The island still had only a few one-lane roads linking everything together. Come to think of it, the roads seemed more like a grouping of wandering paths, not at all laid out for a purpose. A meandering of lanes made for leisurely strolls and scenic trips. There was only one market district with a grocery store, one pharmacy, a town library, and a small police station that never seemed occupied.

We strolled down Quies Street. A small café was open for lunch and we navigated through the few tables scattered throughout the sidewalk.

Jamie leaned into me. Her body gently crashed into mine. "Do you remember our first two weeks here?"

"Yes."

"This place is a bit of a wonder."

"I know." I brought my arm around her shoulder and kept her closer to me. Two small wrinkles on the side of her eyes reminded me of all the time we had spent together. It was nearly thirty years. I thought I had discovered everything about her, but somehow she still found ways to surprise me.

I prayed the treatments would work.

"Michael was our little miracle conceived here," she said.

I smiled. Michael, our son, was the one surprise the island had given us. Jamie was told a few months before our first visit to the island that she would not be able to conceive. We had tried numerous times, but each attempt was unsuccessful. We considered adoption but two weeks of island air and two weeks of island nights gave us Michael.

"We should call him," she said.

"I will. As soon as we come back from the hospital."

"Do you think..." she paused. The look on Jamie's face told me she was concerned about our son.

"I'm sure he'll be fine," I told her but I wanted to bite my lip.

"How long are they going to keep him this time?"

"Not much longer."

"Oh," she said with a reluctant tone.

"He'll be fine," I repeated, not knowing if I was right or wrong. I just wanted Jamie to enjoy our time together.

A single seagull soared high above us. The bird called out once. Its cry sounded like a note played on a broken piano.

"For an island, there really aren't many seagulls," Jamie said.

She was right. I had not noticed a single bird until now.

I remembered our appointment. I looked at my watch. We had twenty minutes until the ferry was scheduled to leave. We were running out of time.

~ * ~

The ferry ride leaving the island took longer than expected. Jamie lost all of her strength on the boat. By the time I drove into the city she could no longer walk. I borrowed a wheelchair from a nurse and brought her into the hospital.

I pushed her through the light green colored corridors. The scent of disinfectant, cleaners, rubbing alcohol, sterile rooms and hospital air that reminds one of illness and death, surrounded me. As a doctor, one never notices the different scents. You forget them. I was no longer a doctor. I was a merely a man taking his wife for radiation treatment. I was only a man hoping that, 'twenty percent chance of recovery' would apply to the woman who had been with me through most of my life.

"I feel so weak," Jamie said.

The words left her lips and pounded my heart like a sledgehammer tearing down the walls of my childhood home.

"I feel so tired."

The words crashed into my chest. In my mind I could see the crumbled remains of a young man's first love falling all around him. Broken memories are the only things that would remain. Memories and an old man left to sift through them.

A door opened in front of us. Dr. Rigo emerged.

"Thomas, I can take care of everything from here. Why don't you go outside for some fresh air," he said.

"I want to be with—" my voice cracked. I was suddenly aware of how cold and wet my cheeks had become.

"Let Jamie and I catch up." Dr. Rigo said with a smile toward Jamie.

I nodded and whispered, "I'll be back in a little while."

"I can call you when we're done," he said.

The door closed. I was left alone in a small waiting room. I sat in a chair in the corner. I waited until my breathing returned to normal, my face felt dry, and my fears left me.

~ * ~

I found a park outside the hospital. It consisted of a small stretch of green grass, and a concrete bench under an elm tree. I sat on the bench and turned away from the hospital.

My cell phone rang.

I fumbled through my pockets until I found my phone.

"Hey Pop," my son said.

"How's everything?" I asked.

"Good," Michael replied.

"You eating well?"

"You sound like mom."

"I guess it's rubbed off on me."

"I ... I got out two days ago." His voice held back a question. I didn't want to know what it was, or what it could be.

"That's good."

"I'd like to see Mom. Actually, see you and Mom."

"Not now. Later." I told him. Jamie wasn't ready and I sure as hell wasn't either.

"I want to visit."

"Right now might not be the best time. We're still getting things organized."

"I could help."

"I don't think it's a good idea," I said. The words came out cold and cruel. I knew it and wished I could have taken them back.

"I've been sober for over a month now." He came at me just as cold. "There are things that I've done that I don't like. I know I've had my share of trouble and a lot of it has hurt you and Mom but I'm not going to lose a chance to be with her a few more times ... before it's too late."

"I can't have you drunk at the house again, Michael. I can't. Not with your mother like this. She doesn't have the strength and God knows I don't have the patience."

"I understand, and I won't be."

His voice was sincere and I knew he was trying but I had heard it all before. "What about the rest of rehab?" I asked.

"My therapist thinks being with mom is a good idea. I think it's crucial. Look Pop, I can't tell you how long I'll stay sober. I can't promise you anything. I can't, but you and I know Mom is dying and I need to be with her just a little while longer."

My son's words brought back the sledgehammer that broke me in the hospital. I felt my eyes sting and my voice give. I held the phone to my ear with nothing to say and without the power to say it.

"We only have a few months left, old man," Michael said.

Michael was stronger than I but I could tell he was on the verge of tears.

I coughed once. My voice came in a whisper. "When are you planning to come?"

"Tonight, if you let me. Tomorrow, if you didn't."

"The last ferry leaves tonight at nine."

~ * ~

Jamie began to feel better once we got back to the beach house. She fell asleep quickly and I was left organizing the remainder of our things.

A little after nine I picked up Michael. He lit up a Marlboro the moment he climbed into the Volvo. We said little to one another on the drive back home.

Once we got to the house, Michael dropped what was left of his cigarette into the soft sand. "Don't worry. I won't smoke in the house." He took the cigarette pack out of his shirt pocket and placed it inside the large duffel bag he brought with him.

We found Jamie happy and as energized as ever. She wanted to cook Michael a meal. He said he was fine but her persistence won in the end. Michael helped and played assistant while Jamie prepared a feast large enough to feed half the island.

Although everything seemed normal—Michael seemed well, and Jamie appeared healthy—I could only eat a few small bites of food. I excused myself the moment they began dessert. I felt they should have some time to catch up. I took a walk down the beach while Michael and Jamie played mother and son.

A storm was on the horizon but the waters on the shore were calm and peaceful. I saw the old man next door prepare his aging boat. I approached him on the shore. I noticed he had several nets and a large harpoon in the small ship. The harpoon was more of a spear with rope tied around the end. I wondered if anyone else used such ancient devices.

"It's a bad night to be out on the beach," the man said with a baritone voice that broke over me like a drowning wave. He looked up. His blue eyes seemed older than the sea.

"Just taking a walk," I said.

He turned his attention back to his boat. He worked coils of rope with hands that had been broken many times. As he tugged at the rope, I could see the signs of snapped bones that had never set correctly under the deformed lumps of sun hardened skin.

"There's a storm out," he said. "You shouldn't be on the beach on nights like this."

"It's out on the horizon. Seems like it's too far out to reach us here."

He looked up at me. "You're the new guy? Just moved in next door?"

"Yes, I am."

"Storms here are a little funny. Sometimes it's best to stay away from the water when the night looks like that." He pointed to the lightning-covered patch of night many miles out on the horizon.

"I'll be going in shortly," I said.

He grabbed hold of the boat by the stern and pushed. The wooden vessel slid over the sand to the water. I watched as he set up the oars and began to row out to sea. When he had moved about twenty yards away from the shore he called out, "You should enjoy this night with your wife and son."

~ * ~

Night drained into early morning. Jamie slept soundly in our bed. Michael rocked back and forth on the small couch, snoring every few turns. Sleep did not come so easily for me.

I walked outside dressed in a pair of old shorts and a white tee-shirt. The beach sand slid through my toes after each step. The sand was not cold as I thought it would be. Instead, it was only a little chilly. I walked to the shoreline where the waves and sand met. The storm on the sea was still far away from where I stood, yet somehow I felt it was closer.

I looked back at my small house. I thought of my sick wife, of my son battling his addiction. I thought of the fisherman alone in the storm. I wondered how he would survive. I wondered if he could survive. I walked out into the small lapping waves. The water felt cool and comforting. I waded until the water was up to my waist. I stood there and let the water hold me. I let my hands drop softly into the ocean. My fingers brushed through the waves as if they were combing the fine hairs of a loved one.

How am I going to make it through all of this?
Something bumped against my thigh.
I looked down.
A white shape swam around me. It wriggled and encircled my legs. The shape was almost six feet long.
I froze.
It moved again. This time, the light of the moon hit the shape. I expected something like a shark but this

had a woman's body. It twisted like a fish but was human.

Who else is out here?

Something else bumped me from behind.

I turned.

Another white human form curved behind me. This one seemed more like a man.

"What the—" the words left me but were cut off.

The first figure came up out of the water. She was pale as death.

I was too scared to breathe.

This thing had Jamie's face. Her eyes, lips, nose. Everything that was my wife only it was dead. A lifeless copy. It was Jamie as I'd seen her in my nightmares. The cancer finally winning. Blue veins covered most of its body.

Something erupted from the water behind me.

I turned.

The second figure was Michael. At least, it had his features but his face was deformed. Twisted and demonic.

"You're going to drown old man," it said.

Claws grabbed my torso and yanked me down.

I caught one last gasp of air before being pulled under the water.

I fought. I punched, kicked and pulled. All in vain.

The two things that grabbed me had their claws in deep and swam with the speed of demons sent to steal souls.

No. Please no. Don't let me die. Don't let me die like this. They, they need me. Michael and Jamie. They're still alive. These things. These things pulling me are not. God, please. I fought. I punched one in the face. I think it was the male. Its skull gave. *Cartilage. It's made of cartilage.* I pushed again.

The figures took me deeper underwater.

My lungs burned. I needed air. *Can't ... can't hold out much longer.* I would have to take that one last gasp. Soon. It would be over. I kicked one more time.

Nothing.

I had nothing else in me. My lungs were empty. My will was gone. My life was over. Calm came over me and I was ready to take that last gasp and drown.

I'm sorry Jamie. I'm sorry Michael.

I hit something. It was hard and stopped me in my tracks. *Ropes. Hard ropes, all around me. Tangling me. A net. A fisherman's net.*

I held my breath longer than I would have thought was humanly possible. Something was pulling me up out of the ocean's depth. Out of the sea.

"Hold on!" I heard him say from above. It was the old man.

He had caught me in one of his nets and was pulling me up to the surface. I made it above the waves. My lungs erupted. I took in as much air as I could. My chest expanded. I breathed again. This time, taking in some water as well.

The fisherman pulled me up into his boat. I coughed and spit out the salt water that tore at my throat.

"Calm down," he shouted.

I pulled and pushed at the net while still coughing up water. My body hurt with each inhale and burned with each exhale.

I twisted to find a way out of the net.

"Stay still." The old man eyed something in the water and threw out a net.

Something splashed.

He grabbed his harpoon, stood on the bow of the boat and threw out the spear. It caught something. He tugged at the rope and then tossed out another net. He yanked at the net and brought a large white shape out of the water. The harpoon was stuck in the thing's side. It twitched a while at the bottom of the boat behind the fisherman and then stopped moving.

The animal caught in the first net was still fighting to find a way out.

The fisherman yanked the harpoon out of the creature in the boat and then hurled it into the other animal in the water.

A scream came. The sound was of an animal unlike I had ever heard. A creature that did not belong on this earth. Its cries ran through me, piercing like a knife cutting my soul. My skin bubbled over as my hairs stood on end.

The fisherman grabbed hold of the harpoon and twisted the wooden pole.

The creature gave out one last gasp and a slight sigh that lead me to believe it was female.

The fisherman clutched the net and brought the thing up into the boat. He threw another mesh over both creatures and then covered them with a tarp.

I found a way out of my netting. I let the rope webbing drop to my feet and I sat at the stern of the boat. I glanced at the two creatures at the bow.

"It's not good to be out at night when there's a storm on these waters." The fisherman grabbed the oars. He sat in front of me and began to row toward the island.

The things had pulled me 200 yards from the shoreline. I said nothing as the fisherman rowed. I had questions. Many questions but when I looked at the old man, his eyes made it clear. Don't ask.

When we got closer to the shore, I wanted to say a million things. The look on his face stopped me before a single word could leave my lips. His expression was simple. You don't want to know.

We made it to shore. I stood. The fisherman sat still in the boat.

"Go back to your family," he said and he waited in his boat until I had left the beach and walked to my house. Once I was inside, I saw him drag the two things he had caught up into his tiny shack.

~ * ~

Jamie and Michael slept soundly while I paced the rooms of the beach house. I looked out of the kitchen window to the fisherman's shack. I had questions. Many, many questions. My mind ran wild as day slowly approached. Near sun up, exhaustion caught up with me. I passed out while sitting at the kitchen table, looking out at the ocean.

~ * ~

"Thomas, Thomas, wake up," Jamie said.

I looked up at her.

"We have to go see Dr. Rigo."

"What?"

"We need to see Dr. Rigo. He called me this morning. Something's happened."

"What is it?"

"He ran some tests yesterday. The tumor's shrunk to less than half the size it was three weeks ago. He wants to see me again today."

I was shocked, scared and excited at the same time. I tried to stand but pain shot through my side.

"What's wrong," Jamie asked.

"I don't know. My side hurts."

I looked down. My shirt had been torn.

"Thomas, what happened to you?"

"I don't—"

"You've been cut."

I lifted my tee-shirt. Under the tear there were several gashes. *Last night. The "things." They ... they were real.*

"What happened?" she asked.

I felt faint. I looked for excuses not to tell Jamie what happened. "I fell on some rocks on the beach last night."

"Well, I'll have Dr. Rigo take a quick look at you today."

"Jamie, I'm fine."

"I want to make sure that—"

"I'm a doctor myself. It's only a scratch. I'll be fine."

I rose, doing the best I could to hide the pain. I looked at Jamie. For a moment, the thing that nearly drowned me last night swam through my thoughts.

"Are you okay?" Jamie asked.

"Yes. Just eager to get going. Where's Michael?"

"He's walking around the island. I think he went for some groceries."

I walked to the bedroom, grabbed some presentable clothes and changed in the bathroom. I looked at the scars on my torso. Two large sets of claw marks lay over my ribs. One gash ran from the back of my shoulder to my hip. The wounds were covered with dried blood. The scabs were breaking in small areas. I cleaned, then, dressed the wounds. I hid the dressing with a plain white shirt and then I put on a button up Polo shirt. I did not want Jamie to see any signs of last night's incident.

My ripped shirt sat on the bathroom counter. Blood stained the areas where the creatures had grabbed me. I seized the shirt, balled it up, and marched to the kitchen. Jamie was getting a few things ready. She did not notice me slide past her. I opened the wastebasket under the sink and was about to toss the shirt away.

I paused.

Inside the basket rested a full pack of cigarettes.
Why would Michael throw those out?

I heard Jamie walking toward the kitchen. I stuffed the shirt in the bottom of the wastebasket.

"You ready to go?" she asked.

"Yes. Just waiting for you."

I glanced outside the kitchen window. The fisherman was patching a broken board on the stern of his boat. He looked up.

~ * ~

Dr. Rigo had no answers. He had no clue as to why the tumor had diminished in size. He told us not to get excited. There were more tests that needed to be done. More results to wait for. Dr. Rigo had his share of questions. I had mine.

~ * ~

Jamie was as energetic as ever. She was healthy, happy and full of spirit. On the trip back home, she played and smiled. She had become the young woman I had fallen in love with so many years ago. I had not seen her like this in many years. She mentioned that I was too stiff. That I needed to relax.

I tried to pretend that things were normal. At least, for her sake. I tried but could not tell if my act was working or if she read right through me.

Once we arrived at the beach house, we found Michael had prepared a meal for us. We sat at the kitchen table like a family for the first time in a long while.

Toward the end of the meal, Michael poured us a glass of nonalcoholic wine. "It's expensive grape juice," he said. "A meal just isn't the same without an after dinner drink."

Jamie smiled.

"Strange thing happened today." Michael cleared his throat. "I ... I woke up without a single thought of drinking. It didn't even come up while I was at the grocery store. I walked past the beer and wine section and overlooked the entire aisle. I only thought of it when I remembered how much you two liked red wine at the end of a meal."

"That's great Michael," Jamie replied.

I said nothing. I only thought of the thing that had yanked me under the water last night. How much it looked like my son. How much it sounded like him.

"Oh, pops, I got some bad news for you," Michael said.

"What's that?"

"I tried to get some fishing done in the afternoon."

Adrenaline shot through me. My hands began to shake.

"I couldn't catch a damn thing," he said. "I asked a few people around town and apparently this is one of the worst places for fishing. It looks like the only guy who has any luck is our neighbor. You might want to ask him what his secret is."

~ * ~

At night, as my wife and son slept, I stared out at the sea. There was another distant storm out in the ocean. The fisherman's boat was gone. The old man was out there, in the storm.

Early morning he returned. His nets were full.

~ * ~

The next few days I traveled with Jamie and Michael throughout the island. Jamie did not feel sick. Michael did not light up as much as a single cigarette and I'm quite sure he didn't have a drink. As we walked through the little town, I looked at the people of Otium Island and noticed several peculiarities. I saw no signs of illness. Even simple things that would be obvious. Things like obesity, or osteoporosis had vanished from this place. Other crippling diseases that would affect the elderly were also nonexistent. As a doctor, my personal opinion was that the people here were too healthy.

At night, I would watch the fisherman. Each night he would go out in his small boat to another storm that never seemed to reach the shores. Once in a while, there were no storms. Once in a while, the old man would simply sit outside and stare off into the ocean, waiting.

~ * ~

Weeks passed and my wife was cured. My son was sober. I remembered our first stay on Otium. Michael was born because of this place.

I did some research and found that there was only a single death on Otium in the last fifty years. Anyone else who had died that lived on the island had done so, away from Otium. In fact, there only seemed to be one death every so many years and it always occurred to a single fisherman.

It was obvious to me why we were so blessed. Why the whole island was blessed. The fisherman protected us. He guarded us from our sins and our suffering. There was only one question that remained in my mind. How could I ever repay him?

~ * ~

Two full months had passed. Life was bliss. I felt a peace that I never dreamed could exist. Then, a storm came. The first storm to reach the island. Rain poured for hours. The wind pounded and howled. Every so often certain cries could be heard from things I knew could not exist.

There was no sign that the storm would subside. I knew something had happened to the old man.

I told Jamie and Michael to wait for me and I raced out of the house. I pushed through the weather and could see in the distance, under the crashing waves that tore at the shoreline, white shapes looking back at me. Waiting for me.

I broke down the fisherman's door, raced through the small house and found the old man on his bed. His body, cold and lifeless. He had probably passed several hours ago when the storm first touched the island. His body wore the signs of a man that had fought to protect the things he loved with all of his soul. Many of his bones had been broken. Cancer engulfed most of the skin on his face and arms. I don't know what had finally taken him. Whether it was cancer, his heart, or a battle on the sea. All I knew was that he was gone. He had passed and there was nothing that I, a doctor, could do.

I looked down at the floor. Several nets were prepared. A harpoon lay beside them. As I looked at these things I realized that Otium Island had never needed a doctor. It would never need a doctor. What Otium Island needed was a fisherman.

High Stakes

"The rules are simple," Tony said as he tossed a deck of cards down on the table in front of us. "We each draw a card. The one with the lowest value card loses."

"I don't have any more money," Jack said.

"Don't worry, it won't cost you a dime."

That caught our attention. Jack and I both rose out of our slumps at the mention of any game that wouldn't put us further in the hole. Of course, when you're in a hotel room after a horrible night of gambling, almost anything sounds good.

"What happens to the loser?" I asked.

Tony chuckled for a second then replied, "The other two punch him in the face."

"You're crazy," I said.

Tony turned toward Jack. "How much are you down tonight?"

"Six hundred. Maybe a little more," Jack replied.

Tony turned toward me. "And you."

"A little over a grand," I said.

"Yeah, I'm at about two grand myself," Tony said. "And let me ask you this. We've each lost at least another couple hundred when you think of the room and everything else."

Jack and I both agreed.

"Okay, but here's my other question," Tony said. "You're still itching to go down to the lobby and play again, aren't you? Something inside of you is saying that you can win it all back. You can finish tonight like you planned. You'll come out ahead or that at the very least, you don't want to end it up here in our room before midnight, right?"

He had a point. I wanted to hit the craps table again. It was just a really bad run. I've done 1000 times better in the past. I only returned to the room when I lost all my cash.

"Why punch the loser in the face?" Jack asked. "I mean, out of all the other things to do, why that?"

"Because I'm pissed at myself and at the world for losing the way I did tonight," Tony said. "I just want to hit someone. I don't care who and I don't give a fuck if I get hit back."

"He's got a point," I said. "I'm pissed that I can't go back down there and clean house."

"Maybe this will teach us a lesson," Tony added. "Maybe it will stop us from blowing all our dough again."

We sat around the table, looking down at the deck of cards. We were all gamblers. Each of us had tried to quit several times. I entered rehab twice in my life, and each time, I counted the days between gambling binges. It was like serving hard time. I loved gambling. I've won some times, lost some times but have never been more alive than in the seconds when a pair of dice leave my hand and dance across a felt table.

"Fuck it," Jack said as he sat down at the table. "I'm in. Let's get this thing started."

We all followed suit.

"Okay, we deal and then flip." Tony said. He took the deck of cards in hand and shuffled. He offered the deck to Jack, who cut the cards and then, dealt everyone, including himself, a card.

"Now flip." Tony said.

I had the Jack of Hearts. Jack held a Queen of Hearts and Tony stared down at the seven of clubs.

"Fuck me," Tony said. "Shit, just my luck."

"You sure you want to do this?" I asked.

"My idea. I guess it's only fitting I should lose first," Tony replied.

I leaned back and threw a right cross. It connected with his left eye.

"Damn it. Damn, that smarts," Tony said. He motioned for us to wait with his right hand and then waved at Jack for the next blow.

Jack threw a fast jab that hit Tony's right eye.

Tony clutched his face.

"You okay?" I asked.

"Tony? Tony? What's wrong?" Jack asked.

"Nothing," he replied. He started shaking.

"What is it?" I asked.

Tony's body continued to tremble until he erupted with laughter.

"What's so funny?" Jack asked.

"Look at me," Tony said. "I have two black eyes, don't I?"

"You do," I said.

"You look like a raccoon," Jack added as he started to laugh.

"It looks like I doubled up." Tony said.

This broke us up and we all started laughing.

After a few moments, we gained our composure and returned to the game.

"Next hand?" Jack asked.

"Let's do it," Tony said.

The low cards came and went. We took our punches. We cursed, cried and laughed for the rest of the night. In the morning, we awoke with sores, blood stained clothes and a new hope that maybe, just maybe we weren't going to gamble anymore.

Tony discovered something that night which gave us a little hope. As we drove away from the hotels and casinos, we were leaving a bully, maybe for the last time.

~ * ~

I didn't think about gambling for a while. Maybe a good month or so. Then, I got into an argument with my boss and I found myself wanting to get away from it all. The dice kept hitting snake eyes in my life. Maybe my luck would be different at the tables. Jack and Tony must have felt the same way because in a matter of a few days, we were all heading back to our drug of choice.

Tony booked a room and we all agreed not to go overboard. Just bring what you felt comfortable losing and nothing else. Our intentions were good.

What's that they say about paths paved with good intentions?

Midnight came. I was up. Had a great run. Just amazing, but Tony and Jack weren't doing so well and I felt pressured to make one last run and head out.

I was up nine grand. The best I'd ever played. By the time the guys found me at my table, they forgot about what they lost. They were cheering me on and I was no longer betting for me, I was winning for them.

A cute blonde stood beside me and every time she rolled, she was on fire. I could have sworn she was either an angel or had loaded dice. She could do no wrong. So, when it was her time to roll, I backed up her bet with all of my winnings.

That roll taught me two things. First, she wasn't an angel and second, those dice weren't loaded.

I lost everything. My friends were so upset, they broke the one rule we all agreed on. They started withdrawing money from their credit cards. At the end of the night, we found ourselves back in our room. Each of us in debt nearly five grand and I felt it was all my fault.

The worst thing that happens to a gambler doesn't happen when he loses, it's when he wins. It makes you feel like you can do it again and again. My win that night made the three of us believe we could do it. That only set us up for our fall.

"The rules are simple," Tony said. He placed a hammer on the table and a deck of cards right beside the hammer. "Loser gets a broken finger."

"What? Are you nuts?" I asked.

"No, I'm not," he replied. "We can't stop gambling. Something needs to make us want to stop."

He had a point. I turned to Jack. "What do you think?"

"Deal the fucking cards," Jack said.

~ * ~

Resetting broken fingers turned out to be cheaper than gambling. If Tony came up with his drastic scheme sooner, who knows the amount of money it would have saved us. And, not just money, how about what gambling had stolen from our lives? The lying, borrowing, friends lost, relationships destroyed, you name it. I can recall at least three relationships where my dance with the dice ended an otherwise healthy and happy love affair.

When you gamble the way Tony, Jack and I did, it was hard for friends to understand the mood swings caused by our highs and lows at the casinos, race tracks or poker tables. It gets hard to keep good friends when you're caught in a downward spiral. I guess that's why the three of us got to be so close over the years. If misery loves company, then the lows we shared made us the three amigos. I guess Tony was tired of the lows. He was tired of crawling back from the graves we'd dig ourselves into. His system was working.

~ * ~

Five months passed and I didn't think about going to another casino. The mere mention of one made my bones ache. I didn't hear much from Tony or Jack for that matter. I imagined they were doing just as well. I called Tony one day, just to see what was new and he seemed happy, for the most part. Seemed like he had stumbled onto a cure for gambler's itch.

Time passed. Eight months after our little bone breaking ordeal, I was let go from my job. I got the corporate downsizing excuse. I collected unemployment. The itch to gamble returned. I didn't have the heart to call the other guys. I went at it alone and drove, night after night to every gambling hall I could find. Borrowed cash from family, friends, and anyone else that would lone me some change. I maxed out my cards and hit rock bottom yet, I couldn't stop.

Tony called me at my folks' house. I didn't have the heart to tell him. I hoped he was doing better than I was. As we spoke I discovered that he was bit by the bug as well. He was still working but cards ran him deep into the red. He thought about declaring bankruptcy.

As for Jack, he was gambling as well. His wife got sick of his late nights and lies. She left him. It seemed like our lives ran parallel to one another's.

Tony wanted us to meet. Said he scraped up enough money to stay at one of the hotels by the casinos. He didn't want to gamble anymore. He needed our help and had a proposition for us but we needed to hear it in person.

Friday night came and I bummed a ride with Jack to see Tony. We drove to the hotel with not a single word to say. I mean, how do you start a conversation when both of you are stuck in hell. Hey Jack, heard your wife left you. How's everything else?

What's he going to say? Oh yeah, she left me. Took nearly everything I owned which isn't much when you've pawned half your shit to pay gambling debts.

We found Tony dressed in a suit but looking worse than ever.

"Take a seat." Tony pointed at the couch in the hotel room.

I sat down. Jack followed. It took me a few seconds to realize, this was the same room where we started playing Tony's game. The punch-the-loser-in-the-face game. The thought of Tony laughing his head off after we both punched him came to mind. It made me smile.

"I can't stop gambling," Tony said while pacing before us. "I can't and I have a funny feeling you guys can't either."

We both nodded.

"I've lost more money this last month than I ever have before," Tony said. "I've never been so low in my life. I can't pay bills. I can't borrow cash from anyone else. I'm talking to a lawyer to see how I can declare bankruptcy but I can't even come up with the two grand to get that started." Tony wiped the sweat from his face. "I'm willing to bet whatever else I have that you both are in the same boat. Or at least something so close to it that doesn't matter who tells the story, it would all sound the same. Am I right?"

"Yeah, you're right," I said.

Jack nodded.

"Well, what if I had a way of changing that?" Tony asked. "What if we could stop gambling or be so horrified by it that we'd never want to do it again?" He looked right at Jack. "What if you'd never have to lie to your wife about where the rent went that month?" He turned to me. "What if you could walk through a casino, step past the craps tables and feel like you never had to roll another seven ever again?"

He had my attention.

"How?" Jack asked.

"We up the stakes," Tony replied. "The last time we played our little card game after a bad night of gambling seemed to help, right? I mean, I didn't want to play for months and I didn't even think about it."

"Same here," I said.

"We have to do something," Jack said. "I can't keep living like this. Christ, I've never felt so low in all my life. Part of me wants to climb to the roof of this building and make a damn nose dive onto the street. Another part of me wants to head right down to the Black Jack table and see if I can make anything happen with my last twenty bucks."

"What are you thinking?" I asked Tony.

"The rules are simple." Tony dug out a revolver from his coat and put it down in front of us. He then fumbled through his pockets and pulled out a single bullet. He placed the bullet right beside the gun. "Russian Roulette. Loser teaches the two remaining gamblers how give up the habit, once and for all."

Passed Out

My hands, tied. Same as my feet. I'm ... I'm trapped. Can't move. Everything's black. What happened? Where am I?

Can't move. Can't. Lying on my back. I'm in a box.

What happened? The party. The girl. Her and her friends must have slipped something into my drink.

What's going on? I ... I'm in a box. It's just large enough where I can fit but can't move.

I hear them. The girl. Her and the others. They're laughing.

"This isn't funny," I yell.

They laugh some more. Something lands on top of the box. It's ... it's dirt.

Oh God, they're burying me.

As Promised

The box was nondescript. Just a plain cardboard container measuring 19x12x16. I snatched it off my doorstep. The box weighed almost ten pounds. Nothing marked on the package gave me a clue as to whom had sent it or what it contained.

I opened the door to my apartment, brought the box inside and set it on my kitchen table. After a few moments of staring at it, I tore the box open.

A Remington 7 typewriter glared back at me from inside. A relic dug up from the 1930s. It had black plastic key tops with ivory white lettering in courier font and a long, horizontal carriage-return lever rather than a short, vertical one. The midnight black surface glistened like a cobra's skin.

A small note taped to the keys read: It is time to own up to your promises.

I was instantly furious. Someone had called me out. Finally, after years of telling people, "I'm a writer," someone had called my bluff.

Bastard. You son of a ... who? Who could it have been?

I thought long and hard but after nearly an hour, I realized it was useless. There were too many possibilities. The truth was that whoever sent the typewriter was right. After all, I was a clerk in a library. That was my real job. Several years earlier, I had set out to write. Create that bestseller. Capture on the page—desire, pain, joy, and agony. Write about the worlds only a writer could visit. See the world as only a writer could see.

In the beginning, I tried. I took a job in the city's largest library. I read the masters. Spent nights dreaming about the writer's life. Eventually I told myself, "Say that you're a writer. Get that out there. Say it. Believe it. It will eventually happen."

Day after day. Year after year. I found being a writer was easy. You just had to tell people you were a writer. After all, it wasn't like being a cop. No one would ask to see your badge. No, as a writer all you had to do was say you were working on your novel. You could say anything and people believed you.

If anyone asked to see your work, you merely said it was not ready. At parties, being a writer was the best icebreaker. Who wouldn't want to talk to a writer? Who wouldn't want to socialize with an intellectual?

As time went on, I discovered more tricks that helped me be a writer. I memorized snatches of description from forgotten authors. I committed poems to memory. Whenever necessity called, I borrowed from another writer and quoted something eloquent and fitting for the moment. A tailored suit of words fit for any occasion. It worked like a charm.

Yes, being a writer was easy. In fact, one of the easiest things I had ever been.

Writing, on the other hand, was hard. Too hard.

After twenty years of being a writer, I found writing to be the most difficult thing one could do. The work was terrible. The pay was worse. The hours, long and lonely. No, I loved being a writer but not writing. After all, writing was work. Being a writer was fun. I preferred being a writer to writing.

I looked down at the note.

It is time to own up to your promises.

I might have promised people things. Promised them it would happen. Promised I would write. Promised myself I would own up to my words, eventually.

I took the typewriter out of its box. Set it on the table and discovered a small stack of paper underneath. I placed the pages beside the typewriter. Then, I took a seat and thought, why not?

I placed the note beside me as a reminder. I lifted the typewriter's bail and loaded a single sheet.

A strange, low chuckle escaped the machine.

A small latch opened just below the space bar. A two-inch thick metal spike shot out from the machine. It pierced my chest. The spike cut through my body, severing my spine just below my sternum and impaling me to the back of the chair.

I tried to scream. A faint whisper escaped—the sound of air leaving my lungs like a balloon slowly deflating.

Four black claws emerged from underneath each corner of the typewriter. They gouged into the table.

I tried to push away from the machine.

No use. The typewriter had me. There was nowhere to go. Nothing left to do.

I looked over at the note beside me.

It is time to own up to your promises.

As I hit each key, a steel arm swung out from the spike that connected me to my chair. The arm quickly withdrew, taking with it pieces of bone, muscle, and tissue. The arm snapped the characters onto the page. Each letter stained its imprint on the white sheet with my blood. The machine became a part of me, a parasite living off its host.

~ * ~

There is a pool of red at my feet. I don't know how much longer I have. I don't know when it will be done. Before I have completed my first work of art. My first tale. I know that it is time for me to own up to my promises. It has finally come. I must write. I must capture on the page—desire, pain, joy, and agony.

I am numb now. I can't feel the arm swing out of my chest any more. I have no regrets. Well, maybe just one, I should have written years ago.

Everything is fine. I am resigned to my fate. I accept it. There is only one thing that bothers me. Actually, two things. Two little words that I know must be written.

The End

Charlie's Invitation

Charlie stood on the ledge. The tips of his shoes hung over the edge as he looked down. The building must have been forty stories, easy. Overlooking the city, Charlie took in a deep breath. He pulled the envelope from his pocket, held it and rubbed it once more. He needed to know it was real for the hundredth time. The heavy card stock pressed into his fingers told him it was.

Charlie placed the envelope back in his pocket and jumped.

He hit the sidewalk with such force that the concrete cracked where his head landed.

A crowd around him formed as strangers held their breath waiting for someone to say or do something.

Charlie stood.

Everyone gasped.

A bone stuck out of Charlie's arm.

People pointed and whispered to one another.

Charlie looked at the bone spiked out of his arm and pulled his wrist. He reset the bone and then walked to work.

~ * ~

During his lunch hour, Charlie walked to a nearby park. He sat on an empty bench, removed the envelope from his pocket and placed it on his lap. He ran his fingers along the envelope and took his time turning the invitation in his hands. He needed to know it existed and that it wasn't a strange trick played on him by his mind. Once he knew it was real, he removed a revolver from his pocket and placed the barrel of the gun in his mouth.

He glanced down at the envelope and pulled the trigger.

The explosion from the gun froze everyone in the park. They stared at Charlie with horrified eyes.

Charlie removed the gun from his mouth and tucked it under his shirt. He placed the envelope back in his pocket, pushed the pieces of his skull back into his head. He then brushed his hair with his fingers, covering the exit wound in the back of his head with his long locks and walked back to his office.

~ * ~

After work Charlie went home and took a long bath. While in the tub, he glanced up at the envelope he had taped on the wall and slit both wrists. Once the blood left his body and turned the bath-water red, Charlie stood, dried himself off and stitched the cuts in his arms back together.

He removed the envelope from the wall, carried it with him to his bedroom and placed it on the bed beside his black suit. He got dressed, put the suit's jacket on over his white shirt and called for a cab. He then removed a length of rope from his cabinet and hung himself from a beam in his room.

Charlie dangled from the ceiling, looking down at the envelope on his bed. When he heard a car honking outside, he cut himself down, tucked the envelope in his coat pocket and went outside to where the taxi stood waiting.

Charlie entered the cab.

"Where to?" asked the cabbie.

Charlie reached into his coat pocket, removed the envelope, opened it and read the invitation.

You are cordially invited to the wedding of Mark Vinco and Ann Smith, to be held on…

He stopped at Ann's name and held his breath.

"Where to?" asked the cabby once more but in a harsher tone.

Charlie skimmed the rest of the invitation and found the address. He told the cab driver the details and tucked the envelope back into his pocket.

~ * ~

Charlie snuck into the church and sat in one of the pews at the rear of the building. He waited patiently for the ceremony to begin. He could see Mark, the groom, waiting at the head of the church.

An organ bellowed out the starting notes of *Here Comes the Bride*.

Charlie turned his head.

Ann walked up the center isle dressed in a white dress that suited her perfectly.

Charlie looked at her one last time. His body quivered and he tried to hide the shakes.

Ann turned and glanced at Charlie. She smiled with sincerity, as if to thank him for coming.

Charlie tried to smile back but seeing her like this was too much. He nodded, clutched the invitation in his pocket and felt his heart finally give.

After all his failed attempts at taking his own life, a smile from a beautiful bride finished the job.

Charlie died watching Ann leave him forever.

Found Doll

I thought about my wife as I looked out the train's window. I had gotten used to the shakes and vibration of the passenger car and my mind came back to Ashley. We were married nearly ten years. As the English countryside rolled before me, I watched hills marry valleys, and small villages dance with life then vanish. Life had its ups and its downs and its spaces of nothing in-between. God, how I hoped for the ups but, with Jessica our seven year old daughter asleep beside me, I would have settled for a whole lot of the nothing in-between.

Ashley was sick. There was nothing else I could do. Nowhere else for me to go. Get away. Get as far away from the States as possible for Jessica's sake. For mine as well.

This was the time to do it. Ashley went back into rehab. There was a job offer as a copy editor for GQ based in Britain for the magazine's European edition. I would have to make the switch from fulltime writer to fulltime editor but considering my other options, I was looking forward to the change. Besides, I was sure I could fit in a few articles of my own whenever the opportunity arose.

Jessica shifted her weight and leaned into me. I smiled down at her. When we left the States I told her we were going on a vacation and that mommy was going to stay behind for a while to rest. It had been the same excuse I used every time Ashley was committed.

Jessica was bright. I'm sure she knew there was a good chance we were never going home again. It was the first time I had seen her sleep soundly in over a year.

Ashley's addiction had sucked the life out of me. For the last three years I did what I could to keep us together but her relapse followed recovery like day followed night. I had lost myself in her addiction no differently than she had, except I didn't cling to drugs and alcohol. I clung to shrinks and therapists, counselors and false hope. It was my daughter who realized I had hit bottom. Ashley disappeared for a weekend. The experience drained all of my energy. I collapsed on the couch with the phone glued to my hand. I awoke to my own sobs and to Jessica's embrace. "Daddy, mommy's sick. It's not your fault," she told me.

At that moment, my daughter became my salvation. From there on, I realized I had to be hers. What would have happened to me if Jessica was not in my life? What if I would have had another daughter or no daughter at all?

The train veered through a valley. I caught a glimpse of a shepherd asleep under a tree. I smiled for a moment. Maybe the nothing in-between was something people looked forward to their whole lives.

~ * ~

I awoke to Jessica's gentle shake. "Daddy, look." Jessica cradled a porcelain doll in her arms. She tipped the doll up and began to laugh.

"What is it honey?" I asked.

"This doll. It's funny. Look." Jessica brought the doll to me. The figurine resembled a six month old girl in a white dress that appeared to come from a long forgotten century. Jessica tilted the doll's head up and as she did the doll's eyes opened and then, under the corners of her mouth a pair of fangs grew.

Jessica laid the doll back down and the fangs retracted.

"She has funny teeth." Jessica brought the doll up again and just like before, she opened her eyes and two sharp pointed canines emerged.

"Where did you find that doll?" I asked.

"There." Jessica pointed to a compartment underneath the seat across from us. "While you were sleeping I started looking around. I tried to be quiet so I wouldn't wake you."

"That's nice of you honey."

"Can I keep her?"

"She might belong to another girl."

"But I didn't see any other little girls on the train."

I thought for a moment. The doll was obviously a gag gift. It probably belonged to a young college kid who read too much Ann Rice.

"Can I?"

I didn't have the heart to turn her down. "I'll tell you what, if no one else comes for it by the end of our trip, you can keep it."

Her eyes lit up.

"But if someone asks for it back, we have to give it to them, okay?"

She nodded and smiled then hugged the doll as tightly as she could.

I glanced at the porcelain figure. Some people have strange tastes.

~ * ~

We arrived at the London flat the magazine arranged for us. It was a tight two bedroom but nice. The neighborhood was quiet. My editor had told me I could stay there if I wished or if I wanted a larger place, he would do what he could to accommodate me.

Jessica got used to the apartment and even though she never mentioned it, I felt she was happy to have peace in her life.

I allowed her to keep the doll she found on the train. No one had asked for it and I thought the owner of the figure would not miss it enough to return to the station.

~ * ~

A scream tore me from my sleep. The cry came from Jessica's bedroom. I rushed to see her.

"What's wrong?" I asked.

Jessica clutched her doll tightly in her arms. Her eyes were shut and from the small twitches her muscles made, I knew she was still asleep.

"Jessica?"

She couldn't hear me.

"Jessica." I squeezed her shoulder.

Startled, she pushed me away. Her eyes opened covered in tears.

"What's wrong, Jessica?"

"Screams … screams."

"Jessica?"

"They all were screaming."

"Jessica, you had a nightmare."

"No. The screams. I could hear them."

"It was a nightmare, baby. Just a nightmare." I tucked her in. "Do you want me to stay here until you fall back asleep?"

"Okay."

I stayed there with her. The moonlight outside kept us company as I reminded myself that turning a chapter in a book is different than turning one in real life. Flipping a thin page is much easier than saying farewell to a part of your past.

~ * ~

In the morning I had a meeting with the managing editor. We discussed the magazine's future and my role in helping it reach its goals. My duties and responsibilities were spelled out and I received a brief introduction to everyone else in the office.

I picked Jessica up from the babysitter my boss recommended and arrived home late in the evening. We were able to sit down and have a nice family meal, something we forgot how to do over the last few months.

~ * ~

"Help me!" Jessica cried.

I jumped out of bed and raced to her side.

She was curled up in a ball and was holding on to the doll.

"What is it?" I asked.

"Help."

I shook her. "Honey, are you okay?"

She opened her eyes. "Blood. There's so much blood."

"Where?" I looked all round but everything in the room was in order.

"Blood."

"You had a nightmare, sweetie. That's all."

"Daddy, they were eating people."

"Who?"

"The family. The family was eating people."

"Baby, you had a bad dream."

"They were…"

I rubbed her back. This soothed her. "Is that better?" I asked.

She nodded.

I glanced down and saw the doll. As Jessica moved, the doll's fangs grew.

I pulled the doll away from her.

"What are you doing?" she asked.

"I want to put the doll away for you."

"But I like it. She tells me stories."

"Well, for tonight, she's going to stay with me." I went to Jessica's toy chest and found a Raggedy Ann doll. "See what stories this one will tell you."

"But I want the other one."

"I know baby, but for tonight, I don't want her around you. She might be giving you the nightmares."

I took the doll into my room and set it on the dresser. As I propped it up, the eyes opened and two fangs grew from under her smile.

"No. I'm not going sleep in this room with you looking like that." I laid it down. The fangs retracted as the eyes closed.

~ * ~

The king sat on the thrown embellished in fine linens. His queen sat beside him. They sat as still as could be. Their pale skin glowed and both appeared to be statues.

I could smell damp earth all around me. It choked the air of life and made the stone building we were in seem like a coffin.

Servants lined up before the king. They brought silver trays with ornate carvings that covered the platters. The servants removed the platters' lids. Red meat lined with fruit filled the plates.

The king shook his head, no.

The servants rushed the platters away. Other servants returned and took their places. They lined up and waited.

A third row of servants entered. This group held a young man whose hands were bound. They brought the man before the king.

The king nodded.

A servant pulled out a long knife while the others held the bound man still.

The servant slit the man's throat. Blood rushed out of the wound.

The king smiled.

~ * ~

I awoke. The dream was still fresh and my heart raced because of it. I wanted to throw up. The vivid details spun around my head. It was as if I were there. As if, I was one of the servants, waiting on the king's wishes and desires.

Chills ran through my body.

I sat up in bed and noticed the doll on my dresser. It was sitting, with its eyes open and fangs out.

My flesh curled at the sight.

I picked up the doll and set it in a box inside my closet. That damn thing was giving me nightmares now. Who would make such a doll? More importantly, who would own such a thing?

~ * ~

The next day was uneventful. I felt normal for a while. Then the doll and the dreams crept back into my thoughts. It's been years since I had any sort of nightmare. At least, any nightmare I could remember.

I told myself it was probably anxiety caused by the recent changes. I had a new job and I was starting a new life with my daughter in a different country. I had a lot to deal with. It was only natural that I'd have some negative emotions manifest themselves in some manner.

~ * ~

Jessica was starting to like the new world we were in. She told me so over dinner. I felt relieved that she was enjoying the change. It made me feel like I was doing something right.

After dinner we played a couple of board games and then got ready for bed. She didn't ask about the doll and I didn't plan on moving it from its secret hiding spot. I tucked Jessica into bed and then I prepared for sleep as well. The door to the closet was closed. I reminded myself that it was just a doll.

~ * ~

The king sat at a large wooden table inside a great banquet hall. It appeared as if we were in a large castle. The table was lit by candles that cast strange shadows on the walls. The black and gray shapes looked like demons dancing all around us.

Servants lined the table. They brought gifts for the king but he ignored them.

A new line of servants came bringing with them a young woman. She was blindfolded and her hands were tied.

The servants lifted her in front of the king and laid her down on the table.

The king grinned. He had two long fangs that poked out from each corner of his lips. He hunched forward and bit the girl's throat.

I moved back.

The king looked up. He glared at me with glowing eyes.

I jumped out of bed, covered in sweat. My heartbeat lessened as I realized I was back in my room and not in some ancient castle.

The nightmares were ridiculous. I wanted them to stop. I turned my head toward the closet and discovered that the door was open.

I walked to the closet and peeked inside. The box I had placed the doll in was open and the doll was missing.

I walked outside the closet and was shocked to find the doll, sitting on the dresser, with its eyes open and its fangs down.

I had enough of the doll. I picked it up and carried it into the kitchen. I placed it in a bag and set it on top of the refrigerator.

I went into Jessica's bedroom. I found her asleep but I needed to know why she was moving the doll around so, I woke her.

"I haven't done anything," she said.

"You didn't go into my room and move your doll?" I asked.

"No. I've been sleeping."

Jessica wasn't the type of girl who told stories or pulled practical jokes. Either she was lying to me now or, I was moving the doll myself and forgetting about it, or … well, I didn't want to think of the other option. I decided to go back to bed and deal with the situation in the morning.

~ * ~

After work I brought the doll to a doll maker I found online. He specialized in porcelain dolls that resembled antique pieces. When I spoke to him over the phone he wanted to see the doll.

I dropped the doll in front of him and he immediately was drawn in by its uniqueness.

"Where did you get it?" he asked.

"I found it on a train. Actually, my daughter did," I replied.

He picked it up and tugged at the doll's clothing. "May I?" he asked.

I nodded.

He then pulled some of the clothing apart to see how it was assembled.

"Have you ever seen anything like this?" I asked.

"Not exactly." He seemed too lost in the doll to look at me.

"What do you mean?"

"Doll makers have been asked to make all sorts of dolls, and through the years, technology has been there to help us. So, if you're asking me if I've ever seen a doll that resembled a vampire, then yes. But if you're asking me if I've ever seen a doll like this one, no. This doll is very, very old."

"How old?" I asked.

"I don't know but she's old. Look at the joint in the doll's arm." He pointed to the doll's shoulder. "Most joints on modern dolls are plastic or have rubber links. Some could be pieced together with thick rubber bands. Some older dolls used coiled springs but this one has wooden rings around the joints and is held together by some type of rope."

I looked and saw the wood joint that protected the porcelain arm.

"You have a very rare and very old doll here," he said as he dressed the doll. "Look at the fabric used for the doll's dress." He lifted the doll up to me. "I would guess this fabric was made at least 200 years ago."

He turned the doll up, opening its eyes and making its fangs appear.

"This is a very special piece," he said. He set it down on the counter and stared at it for a while before facing me again. "How much do you want for it?"

"You'd buy the doll from me?" I asked.

"Yes."

"I wasn't thinking about selling it. I just wanted to find out a little more about it."

"I'll give you three thousand pounds, right now. "

I thought about his offer. I didn't like the doll being in the house. I was tired of the nightmares and after the brief history lesson on doll making, I was even less inclined to take it back with me.

I extended my hand. "You have a deal."

~ * ~

I left the doll maker with a wad of cash in my pocket. The money was nice but getting the doll out of the house for good, was a blessing. No more nightmares. No more worries. The only thing that got to me as I made my way home was a nagging question.

Who originally owned the doll? I couldn't put a face to the owner of the porcelain figure.

~ * ~

Night came and I enjoyed my evening with Jessica. Our new little world was having a great effect on her and I started to like our life here. There was something to be said about the moments with nothing in-between.

~ * ~

Days turned into weeks and Jessica and I both forgot the struggles we went through. I heard from the States that Ashley was doing better and I was happy for her. Everything was perfect. Well, everything except for one thing. Every now and then the image of the doll would pop up in my head. I'd see the doll rise, open its eyes and sprout fangs. I tried to shake the image out of my mind and when I did, only one question remained. Who lost the doll?

~ * ~

One night in October, someone knocked at my door. It was after midnight and Jessica was asleep. When I opened the door, I was surprised to find a girl around the same age as my daughter at my doorstep.

"May I help you?" I asked.

The girl said nothing. She stood before me, staring. She had long black hair and pale white skin.

"What's wrong?" I asked.

She said nothing. She stood there and watched me.

"It's late, you shouldn't be out at this hour," I said.

"Where's my doll?" she asked.

"I don't know what you mean."

She looked into my eyes. Her gaze reached down into my soul. I was frozen.

"You found my doll and I want it back," she said. Her eyes glowed and when she smiled, I knew who lost the doll.

The Letter

"Someone left this for you," said Anna, the secretary.

Mike looked up. She was holding a black leather envelope in her hand.

"Who sent it?" he asked.

"I don't know. A messenger stopped by earlier and said he had a delivery for you and that it needed to be delivered today."

Mike took the envelope.

"Was there anything else?" Mike asked.

"He only said that you had to read it today," she replied.

He noticed she looked frazzled. "Anna, is anything wrong?"

She fidgeted with her hands, as if she didn't know where to place them. "The messenger … he was strange."

"How so?"

"Well, I've never met him before. I know all the delivery guys that come up here and this was the first time I ever saw him, yet, he knew me. Like we met somewhere else. I asked him if we've ever run into each other and he said no but there was this feeling."

"I don't know what you mean."

"There was a feeling of familiarity between us. It was strange. He also knew a lot about you."

"About me?" Mike asked.

"Yes. He knew what time you took your break. What time you came in. I mean, almost to the second. It was strange."

"Messengers are usually bizarre people. Maybe he has a vibe you didn't like."

"Well, that was also something I picked up on. He seemed sick. I can't put my finger on it but there was something really off about him."

"Well, that could be it. He's a little off balance. That usually can send people a message that scares them."

"I don't know. It seemed like he was from some other place." She excused herself and closed the door.

Mike's corner office was quiet. It was one of the perks of the job. A workspace, apart from the madness.

Mike sat back down in his chair. He rain his fingers over the envelope and stared at the leather piece. It had no distinguishing marks, with fine stitching around the edge. It looked expensive and grabbed his attention. Whoever sent it knew he'd want to open it the moment he saw the envelope. A single wax seal held the main flap closed.

He pulled the flap open and found a hand written note addressed to him. The script seemed extremely familiar and yet at the same time, foreign. He knew the person who wrote the letter but couldn't, for the life of him, link the script to a face or name.

The note read:
Mike,

The outbreak spreads Monday. Millions will die. You don't have much time. You don't have to believe what you read this moment but shortly, you will. This is all you have. This note and what it tells you to do. Leave everything else behind. You're the key. What you know of reality will change. The unbelievable will become as real as this letter you hold in your hands.

Monday, a contaminated group will be on a boat called the OASIS. It was meant to stop at our harbor but the whole crew became infected. The boat veers off course and crashes into a dam next to the city's water supply. Someone on that boat makes it to the water supply and dies in the lake. The body decomposes and changes the molecular structure of the virus. This mutation makes it impossible to stop. It's believed that the only way of preventing the full-scale spread and mutation of the disease is to stop that boat. You need to destroy it before it hits that dam.

Sunday, the National Guard loses control of the city. Riots consume most of the area. It's near impossible to move on the roads without issue. You'll need to have weapons and ammo yourself. Soldiers will be forced to open fire on anyone who looks sick. Many will die. Some of the infected will display different powers. This will be the first time you'll see the unbelievable.

Saturday, troops are deployed. The pubic goes into a panic. You discovered you're one of the few immune to the illness. There are others like you and then there are others who can carry the virus but don't lose their minds because of it.

Friday afternoon, it starts. You need to stop that boat and prepare for it now. You're entering a world beyond belief and beyond words. You can change things for the better if you stop that boat. If you don't, the virus will become too powerful. By Wednesday, the government will deploy air strikes on most major cities within the United States. Life as you know it, will end. Our society will crumble and only a small number of us will remain. The rest will go mad or die.

Mike

Mike froze. The signature startled him. The letter was his handwriting—when he's rushed or stressed. That's why it looked familiar.

Was someone playing a trick on him? What was going on? He wondered.

Mike glanced down at the note. It had one last message.

PS: Watch out for the plane. Run the moment it hits.

An explosion erupted outside the office. Screams roared outside.

Mike swung the office door open.

"What the hell's going on out here?" he asked.

Smoke and debris littered the office. People ran in all directions.

Mike moved forward. Something had crashed through the building's wall and apparently slid into the middle of the office. Through all the smoke and commotion, he could make out a large round shape. It was a Cessna's engine.

Last Bullet

Five wolves lay dying at my feet. Some cried while others licked their wounds where the silver bullets entered. They all were changing. Their bodies morphed from beast to men.

I held the revolver closer to my heart. One silver bullet was left.

A howl escaped the shadows. Three more wolves emerged. Three more werewolves from the dark of night. One last bullet in the chamber.

I took one long deep breath. Did I make one last kill or turn the gun on myself?

The Tree

Adam let his pickup truck roll to a stop. Lisa, his fiancée, studied a map in the passenger's seat. He held the steering wheel and waited for the light to turn green. A black crow cawed from a wooden fence post. Adam glanced at the bird. Its jet black feathers glowed in the bright sunlight. Adam's eyes traveled from the crow to the corn field behind the bird.

It's just a mile away from here, he thought. *I'm just a mile away from her.*

Lisa tilted her head up. "Green light."

"What?" he asked.

She pointed. "The light's green."

Adam broke from his day dream and stepped on the gas.

"Do you want to pull over?" she asked.

"I'm fine," he said.

"You sure? I can drive the rest of the way if you're too tired."

"We're almost there." Adam caught a glimpse of the billboard announcing his home town. "Look, we're basically here."

Lisa turned her head toward the sign.

Before them stood an aged billboard that read, *Now Entering Damnum County.* Wooden chips were missing from the board and the bottom corners had rotted away. It appeared as if someone had given the sign maybe one fresh coat of paint since Adam left.

"You excited?" she asked.

"Of course I am," he replied.

"She smiled and snuggled up next to him. "I don't mean about the wedding. Are you excited about coming back home?"

"I don't know. I guess it hasn't hit me yet."

Adam glanced in his rearview mirror. He could see the field and thought about her again.

~ * ~

They arrived at the farm house. Everything looked the same as Adam remembered.

The front door opened and his father stepped out as Adam stopped the truck.

Adam smiled at his father.

His father waved back.

This part of the world hadn't changed, it just got a little older.

Lisa jumped out of the truck and approached the old man. She kissed him on the cheek. "It's so nice to meet you."

"My son never mentioned how beautiful you are."

She laughed. "I can see where Adam gets his charm."

Adam followed behind with a set of suit cases. "Dad is charming up until the point where he's yelling at you from the top of a tractor."

"That's because some boys are too hard headed to do things right," replied the old man.

Adam dropped the bags and embraced his father. "How's Mom?"

"She's good and she's waiting inside for both of you. She prepared enough food to feed the whole town. I asked her if we had any other kids I didn't know about with the feast she prepared."

"You know Mom," Adam said. "She wants to make sure everyone's taken care of."

"Well, get on in there and say hello. I'll move the rest of your things into the house."

~ * ~

After dinner, Adam climbed the stairs to his old room. He sat on his childhood bed and let the memories of innocence spring from the corners of his imagination. The toy trucks that rested on his bureau reminded him of long summer days spent outside under the shade of trees. He would pretend to be a truck driver in a world made of sticks, stones and mud pies.

Adam smiled at the thought.

His kite hung from the ceiling. It brought him back to windy days in the field where he saw it first take flight. He remembered making the kite with his father. He laughed at the thought of how a piece of string, a cut up grocery bag and some sticks could turn into a flawless bird capable of performing a perfect take-off.

Stuck in the corner of his dresser's mirror, he saw a photo. Adam walked to the image. It was one of him and Emily. They were ten at the time. They sat under their favorite tree, holding hands and smiling. The picture brought him back to a place that had been buried in the back of his mind.

~ * ~

Emily smiled from the top branch of the large elm tree.

"Don't be scared," she said.

"I'm not," he said from below. He stood on the ground, looking up at the tree. Its branches reached up and outward like a large hand sprouting out of the ground.

"Well, then?" she asked. "Are you coming or not?"

"I'm thinking."

"About what?"

"The best way to get up there."

"You don't think, silly. You just climb," she said with a ten-year-old's smile.

"Well, how do you get down later?"

"I don't know. You just do."

He stepped up to the trunk and paused.

"Do you want me to come down and show you?"

"No."

"Well then, do it. Climb."

Adam reach up, grabbed the first branch and pulled. He grabbed the next and pulled. He didn't think. He took her advice and climbed. A few minutes later, he sat beside her looking out at the world before them.

"See, it was easy," she said. She leaned in and kissed his cheek.

"You can see everything from here," he said.

"We need to mark this spot," she replied. "That way, people will know we were here."

"Wait, I have my grandfather's pocket knife." Adam held onto a branch with one arm and dug deep into his pocket with his other hand. He pulled out a brown pocket knife, unfolded it and then carved Emily's name followed by his into the tree's thickest branch.

"That's great," she said.

"Wait, it's not finished." He continued to carve away until both their names were encased by a heart.

~ * ~

"Adam?" Lisa asked.

He turned from the photo and looked at Lisa standing in the doorway. For a second, he was ten-years-old again and was up in the town's largest tree with the love of his adolescent life.

"Adam, are you okay?" Lisa asked.

He placed the photo down on the dresser and felt the passing of time run through his body. He was no longer a farm boy running around the fields with cute little Emily Nichols from down the street.

"I'm okay." He looked around the room and then back at Lisa. "Lots of memories, that's all."

Lisa entered the room. She looked down at the picture of Emily and Adam. "Is this Emily?" she asked.

"Yeah."

"You're father told me about her," she said.

"He did?"

Lisa placed her hand on his shoulder. "Do you want to talk about her?"

"I don't know."

"Adam, we're getting married in a couple of days. I don't want to have any secrets between us. You can tell me anything."

"Emily isn't a secret. At least, I haven't meant for her to be one."

"You've never mentioned a thing about her." She took his hand.

"I'm sorry." He led her to his bed and they sat down.

"I want to know more about you," she said. "We've been together for four years and it still doesn't seem like I know much."

"Talking about this is hard," he replied.

"Why?"

"Emily meant a lot to me and when I moved away, I tried to leave everything behind me. That's why I don't talk about her, my parents, or the farm."

She rubbed his hand. "Well, you can start now."

"Okay, what do you want to know?"

"Anything. Start wherever you like."

"Emily lived in the next farm over. Her parents and my parents were very close and that made Emily and I grow closer together. She was just a year younger than me. We practically grew up in the same crib. She was my best friend."

"Did you two fall in love?"

"We were too young to know what we felt but I believe we did love each other. I saw her as my first love and up until I met you, my only love. I mean, she was always there for me. That can change the world for a young boy."

"Did you always know that you loved her?" Lisa asked.

"I always felt something for her. I don't know when the emotions became stronger and I don't believe real love is what you see in the movies. Two people don't see each other in a crowded room with sparks flying as they fall madly in love with one another. Real love starts off as a seed. It's as small as a glance, a smile, or a simple hello whispered to you. If it's placed in the right soil and time waters it enough, what stems from years of friendship is love."

Adam stood and went to the window. The last rays of light broke through the hills. The reds and oranges of dusk faded. Adam could see the faint shape of the tree wave to him as night stretched over the land.

"What happened to Emily?"

"My father didn't tell you?" Adam asked.

"He mentioned that she passed away."

"Oh." He stared out into the night. He wondered about the tree. *What does it look like now? Are our names still there?*

"Adam?"

"Dad would put it that way."

"What do you mean?"

"I guess he doesn't like to think about what happened either." Adam returned to the bed and sat beside his fiancée. "Emily's father died when we were young. I think I was twelve. It was hard on her and her mother. My parents tried to help with some of the work but it was impossible to run both farms. Emily's mom eventually found some people who for a few years helped and she turned things around. Things got back to normal. At least, as normal as they could be for a young girl like Emily. A couple of years later, Emily's mother got remarried to one of the men who helped out around the farm."

Adam paused as all the memoires returned.

"Adam?"

He shook his head. "I'm sorry. I ... I just haven't thought about it for a long time."

"What happened?"

"Emily changed. She no longer smiled. She stayed here with me most days. She didn't want to go home. She didn't want to play. I couldn't understand why. Then, the summer before I started high school, Emily got worse. She cried a lot. The day after school started, Emily asked me to meet her by our tree. She called it "our tree" because we were the only kids who ever climbed all the way to the top."

Adam paused. He didn't want to continue.

Lisa placed her hand on his back.

"She wanted me to meet her by our tree," he repeated. "She said she needed to talk. I was trying out for the school football team. Practice got out later than I expected. I arrived at our tree at sun down and found Emily. She ... she had hung herself."

"I'm sorry Adam. I'm so sorry."

"If only I had been there when I said I would. If only I would have blown off practice or left early. Anything at all like that, she would still be alive. It's taken me so long to accept it. I had no way of knowing…" Adam wiped the tears from his cheeks. "I cut her down but it was too late. She left me a note. She didn't want anyone else to read it. She was too ashamed to tell anyone else. I was the only person she trusted. The note said that her stepfather had been abusing her."

Adam shut down. He seemed almost lifeless after telling Lisa the story he'd never told anyone else.

"I don't know what to say, Adam."

"That's why it's been so hard for me to come back home. My parents understood. They never asked me to come back when I went away to school. They understood and came up to see me whenever they could. They'd take a flight at least twice a year, until my mom got sick."

"And this is the first time you've been back since?"

"First time. I wasn't able to deal with things here. The sheriff arrested the stepfather. There was enough evidence to convict him. I thought that after he went to prison, I'd have closure but that wasn't the case. The ordeal took its toll on the whole town. Emily's mother sold the farm and moved away. My parents felt like they lost a daughter as well. I lost my best friend and my innocence the day she died."

"I'm here for you Adam. I want to be here for you, now and forever."

"I'm sorry if I've been moody. I want you to know that I'm happy with you. I guess I haven't thought about these things in a long time."

"Are you okay?" she asked.

"I need to put it past me. It's not fair for you to marry a man who hasn't moved on. I think I'm at that point where I can. You've helped me reach it."

"I know Emily meant a lot to you and your family. I don't want you to stop honoring her and her memory. It was a very sad thing to lose someone under those circumstances."

"Well, I want to let go of it all. I need to. I can't keep living in the past or running from it. I'm glad I found someone so understanding."

"You're worth it."

"No, seriously. Thank you for all of this. I know getting married on a farm isn't every young girl's dream."

"Don't be silly," she said.

"Listen, I know you agreed to this so that my mother could be a part of it. You know how sick she's been. It's meant a lot to me."

She grabbed his hand. "I'm excited. This is a beautiful place."

"I promise you, in a few years we'll renew our vows and you'll have your dream wedding."

"This is my dream wedding. I'm with the love of my life."

~ * ~

The days that followed met Adam with a series of obligations and jobs leading up to the wedding. Lisa's various family members arrived from out of town and Adam had to pick them up from the airport and take them to their hotel. The final details involved catering, flower arrangements, and finally, meeting with the priest. Adam went through the motions. It helped keep his mind off of Emily.

~ * ~

The night before the wedding, Adam stayed awake until the early morning hours. He stared out the window and could see their tree. He wondered if there was a way to put Emily behind him. He worried about becoming a husband and had the normal jitters associated with life's major changes.

~ * ~

Adam stood at the altar with Lisa at his side. A crowd of family and friends gathered around the couple. They stood under a gazebo erected for the occasion. Adam's bride was beautiful.

"Dearly beloved, we are gathered here today," said the priest.

Adam stood still and waited. He looked over the crowd as the ceremony continued. Friends he had not seen in years smiled up at him. He tried to concentrate on them, on the ceremony but he could see their tree staring back at him from beyond the field. It was near dusk. The sky glowed orange and red.

"—in holy matrimony," said the priest.

Adam focused on the wedding once more. He glanced at Lisa and she smiled.

Adam looked at his parents but his eyes returned to the tree. He remembered running around the trunk with Emily. He could feel the bumps and scratches of bark under his hands. He remembered thinking as a kid of the roots. He imagined them to be veins that reached the center of the world. He thought that if the tree was ever uprooted, he would see the Earth's core.

"If anyone here believes that these two should not be joined, speak now or forever hold your peace," the priest said.

Adam could feel the tree calling.

"Wait," Adam said.

The priest stopped.

"Lisa, I can't do this," Adam said.

"What?" she whispered.

"I have to go," Adam said.

Adam stepped down from the gazebo. He made his way through the aisle, keeping his head low, and walking briskly past the rows of shocked family and friends.

Once he reached the field he ran as fast as his could. He sprinted, and when he reached the woods, he never looked back. He wanted to know if the tree still had both his and Emily's names carved in its top branch. He needed to know if that had changed. If time could erase the love of a ten-year-old boy.

The tree had tripled in size. He remembered what Emily told him, *you don't think, silly. You just climb.*

He reached up and pulled. He tugged and stretched and pulled again. He thought of how much Emily knew of not only life, but of love. Her simple climbing lesson affected the rest of his life. He knew that if she were still alive and he asked her, how do you love? She would reply, you just do, silly. You just do.

Adam's adult body couldn't maneuver around the smaller branches. He had to break through them. The branches dug into his flesh, slowing him down. Blood flowed from the gashes but he kept moving.

"How do you forget, Emily?" he asked. "How do you forgive?"

He climbed.

"How do you move on?"

He continued to climb and waited for her to answer.

None came. Instead, another branch slashed through his arm.

"Why has it taken me this long to come back here? Why haven't I been able to return?"

He rose.

"Why haven't I been able to move on?"

He reached the top of the tree. He could see not only the town but his whole life before him. Adam found the top branch and cried when he looked at the carving a boy made many years ago. Emily and Adam encased by a heart. The answers came when he found the inscription beneath it. Someone else had carved out a single word into the branch below the heart.

Forever.

Lostinhorrorhouse.com

Jason walked past his couch potato roommate, Chris, and made his way into the kitchen.

"Chris, you've got to check this out," Max yelled from his bedroom.

Chris sat on the couch staring blankly at the TV. A car commercial played and Chris was too hypnotized to care about anything else.

"Chris, check this out," Max said.

"I'm busy."

"No you're not. Come here."

Chris slouched off the couch and walked from the living room to Max's bedroom. "What is it?"

Max sat at his desk, pointing at his computer. "This is some crazy stuff. "

Lostinhorrorhouse.com was the website. A banner ran across the site warning viewers to think twice before watching. Max clicked 'play.'

"What is this?" Chris asked as the video loaded.

"Just watch."

An exterior shot of a house played on the computer screen. It was night. One small light came from the interior. Two guys dressed in black with dark ski masks circled around the house. A cameraman followed. One of the men found an unlocked window, opened it and waved the other two men over. The two masked men entered. The cameraman moved in behind them.

"What the hell are you guys watching?" asked Jason from the doorway.

"I don't know," Chris replied. "Max found it."

Jason entered the bedroom, joining his two roommates. He held a turkey sandwich in one hand and a diet Coke in the other.

The two masked men entered a bedroom and found an older man asleep. One of the masked men pulled out a long knife. He waved the weapon in front of the camera, nodded to the cameraman, and thrust the blade into the sleeping man's chest.

The old man screamed. He grabbed his chest with both hands.

The knife was pulled from his body and then thrust back in.

The old man gasped.

The stabbing continued until the old man's screaming stopped. The video faded to black. An image popped up from the site. 'Thank you for visiting Lostinhorrorhouse.com. Please come back soon. We'll have more.'

"Isn't that crazy?" Max asked.

"It's sick. That's what it is," Jason replied.

"Come on. It's fake," Chris said.

"You think so?" Max asked.

"Yeah, play it again. It can't be real," Chris said.

"Are you guys that twisted?" Jason asked. "You're going to watch that again?"

Max clicked a button and the video began to load.

"You guys need help," Jason said.

"Don't be a wimp. It's just a prank," Chris said.

"Prank or no prank, it's a video of a guy getting snuffed. Who would want to make such a thing? And more importantly, why would you want to watch it?" Jason asked.

"Come on," Max said.

"I'll leave you two demented morons to your own demise." Jason walked off.

~ * ~

Two weeks later, Lostinhorrorhouse.com had become Chris and Max's nightly entertainment. Each night they would upload a new video, watch it and discuss whether it was real, fake, good or bad. Each video started off the same. An outside establishing shot of a home, apartment, or condo. Then the viewer would see how these men broke into the dwelling and slaughtered its innocent inhabitants. Beheadings. Mutilations. Stabbings, and beatings. A drowning was videotaped when the masked men happened upon a young woman taking a bath.

At the end of the second week, Jason arrived home to discover Max had routed the live feed from the computer to the television set in the living room. Chris sat on the couch with a bag of popcorn.

"What are you doing?" Jason asked.

"Waiting," Chris said.

"For what?"

The television flickered and Lostinhorrorhouse.com popped up on the TV screen.

"You're still watching that sick shit?" Jason asked.

"Yeah, what's the big deal?" Max said as he emerged from his room.

"You're watching people die. Regardless if it's fake. Regardless if it's a prank, or not, it's disturbing," said Jason.

"So?" Max questioned.

"Is something wrong with you? I mean, really?" Jason asked.

Max shrugged his shoulders.

"You don't think this stuff is bothersome? It doesn't bug you that people are doing this and other people, like you two idiots are watching?" Jason asked.

"What the hell is it to you? What do you care what I watch or don't watch?" Max asked.

"Well, I think you should contact the cops or find out a little more about this site." Jason said.

"Guys," Chris said.

"No. It's just a website. A few guys probably just running around making cheap mini horror movies," Max said. "Hell, I think it's creative."

"Guys," Chris repeated.

"Creative? You've lost your damn mind," Jason said.

"To hell with you," replied Max.

"Guys!"

"What?" Max and Jason shouted in unison.

Shaking in his seat, Chris pointed at the video screen in front of him. "It … it's our house."

Recovered

The restaurant slowed as closing time approached. Thomas flipped the piece of steak over in the frying pan. Hot grease jumped from the pan, singeing his arm. Thomas flinched, ground his teeth and watched three blisters rise from where the grease had landed on his forearm.

Thomas thought about the pain. Years ago he would have taken a shot of Jack to soothe the burn. A cook's trick that provided a fast fix and it tasted better than any first aid. The bartenders were always willing to pour you anything at any time. Especially if you're the only cook working at night.

Instead of asking for a drink, Thomas looked at one of the empty seats in the back of the restaurant. He imagined Michelle sitting there, waiting for him with a half crooked smile adorning her beautiful face. He winked at the empty chair and pictured Michelle's smile widen and her brown eyes dance with enthusiasm. He pictured her long dark hair and all of the subtle shades it contained.

The pain in his arm was gone.

Thomas returned to the sizzling steak. He added a pinch of pepper and looked up at the clock on the kitchen wall. It was ten thirty. Half an hour until the kitchen was officially closed. That meant at least one rush of orders and then he could clean up. He would be out by 11:40 and home by midnight.

~ * ~

"She's gone, Thomas," Anthony said.

The words tore through Thomas like a rusty blade.

"What do you mean?" Thomas asked. His hands shook. Thomas did everything he could not to let the phone slip from his hands.

"She's … she died tonight, Thomas," Anthony said at the other end of the line. "A … a drunk driver ran a red light. She died instantly. I thought you should know."

The words left Thomas frozen.

"The viewing is tomorrow. The … the funeral's the following day," Anthony said.

"Thanks for calling."

"She would have wanted you to know," Anthony replied.

The phone fell silent.

Thomas was lost. For once in a long while, part of him wanted a drink more than anything in the entire world.

He remembered the first day he met Michelle.

~ * ~

"Thomas, Thomas Abdo?" Michelle asked.

The mound of dirty flesh half resembling a man looked up from his chair in the waiting room. "Yeah, that's me."

"Come in," she replied.

Thomas entered her office. He slumped down into a couch. "I take it this is where I'm supposed to sit?"

"Yes."

"Great." He wiped his face with a shaky hand.

"Can you tell me why you're here?" Michelle asked.

"It's a little obvious, don't you think?" he replied.

"I'd like to hear it from you."

"Court order. My second DUI. It's therapy or jail time."

"Do you want therapy?"

"I don't want jail time."

A soft, slightly crooked smirk came to her face.

Thomas glanced over her features and began wondering about this woman who wasn't that much older than himself.

"I would like to help you but as a therapist, I cannot change your desire to drink. If you feel that you're here just to please the State, and not to seek help yourself, I won't take you on as a client."

"Maybe we were never destined to be together." He smiled and extended his hand. "It was nice meeting you."

She shook his hand.

"If you don't mind me asking, why do you drink?" she asked.

He had no answer.

"If you ever want to give it up, you need to answer that question," she said. "And if you ever feel that you need help, I'll be right here."

~ * ~

Thomas choked as he approached Brooke's Funeral Home. His thoughts raced with memories of Michelle. He stopped a few yards shy of the entrance and turned around. Behind the parking lot there was a tree surrounded by shrubs. He made his way to the tree without tripping or falling. Once he was hidden, he leaned on the tree. The pain in his gut folded him over. Thomas waited, expecting to vomit. He clutched his stomach with his free hand and waited.

A faint crash of thunder came followed by a soft sprinkle of rain. He was transported to the night many years ago where his affections toward Michelle bloomed. He remembered that night as if it were yesterday.

Rain poured all around her. Thomas could see the outline of her bra through the soft fabric of her white shirt.

"Thomas, are you okay?" Michelle asked. She came into the cabana where he sat. The rainy night made everything a few yards away invisible. The cabana was an island isolating Michelle and Thomas from the rain and the rest of the world. The ocean waves could be heard lapping against the coastline a hundred feet from where they stood. The strip of bars and restaurants half a block away was nothing more than a faded glow of lights.

"He died today, Michelle. The old man died today," he said.

"I'm sorry, Thomas." She stepped back.

He wondered if she could smell the whisky on his breath. "Why do you care?"

"He was your father, I imagine—"

"No, why did you come here? Why did you come see me?"

"You called, Thomas."

"Yeah, but other people wouldn't care what gutter I crawled into."

She smiled.

"Michelle, other therapists wouldn't give a damn what happened to their patients as long as they got paid. Why did you come out here, tonight?"

"Because, my father was a drunk, Thomas. No different than yours. He beat my mother, my brothers and me no differently than your father attacked you and your mother. I know how you feel. I understand and know what you have to face, I've been there."

"I'm sorry," he said. "I never knew."

"Not many people know."

"I'm really sorry."

"It's all right. You don't need to apologize." She squeezed his shoulder. "Do you want to talk about it?"

"I don't know. He's gone and I don't know how I feel. I always thought I'd feel good the day he died. I'd be glad that the rotten bastard finally got his. I can't help but hate him even more now. I don't know. I guess part of me believed he would make it up to us. It never happened. And now, it never will."

"I felt the same way, Thomas. I still do."

"Did you ever forgive him?" he asked.

"No, but I learned to forgive myself. That's all you can do. That's all anyone of us can do."

Thomas looked into Michelle's soft, brown eyes. There was tenderness there unlike any other place he'd ever experienced. Her eyes embraced him as a man and not as a drunk. He felt hope for the first time.

"Do you think there's a chance for me?" he asked.

"A chance for what?"

"To live a normal life and never drink again."

"I know there is." Michelle said.

~ * ~

Thomas entered the funeral home. A crowd of strange faces glanced back at him. He gave a small nod and closed the door behind him. The mourners were strangers, friends, and family that shared Michelle with him. People he never would have met. He thought of the other life Michelle lead. He wondered if anyone else knew about him. Did she ever mention his name or was he a faceless, nameless stranger who came to give his last respects?

Thomas spotted the closed casket at the back of the room. He remembered the first time he told her how he felt.

~ * ~

"I'm in love with you, Michelle. I know this might sound crazy to you, but I'm in love with you."

"Thomas, I'm your therapist," she said. "I understand that you've shared some of your deepest secrets that—"

"Michelle, I'm in love with you. Not because of our time here. Not because of the secrets I've shared with you. I'm in love with you because I'm whole again. I haven't touched a drink in a year. It's because of you."

"Thomas, please," she said. Michelle shifted uncomfortably in her chair.

"I love you. I do."

"Thomas, this happens. Certain feelings are misinterpreted and—"

"There's nothing to misinterpret. I know how I feel about you. I know that I've never felt like this before in all my life."

"Why?" she asked. "Why do you love me?"

"You never gave up on me. When life seemed to bury me under six feet of dirt, you were there. You brought me to life again."

"Thomas, therapy can have that effect on you."

"It wasn't the therapy. It was you. Just knowing that a woman like you exists. That you cared if I lived or died gave me life again. You have a great heart. You saved me."

"Thomas, I don't know what to tell you. If you feel this way about me, then you must see another counselor."

"That's the other thing I came to tell you, I don't need therapy anymore."

"What?" she asked.

"I'm done. I know how this might have turned out. I know you would feel strange about it. I knew there was a chance that you would want me to see someone else but I realize now that you're the reason I stopped drinking all together. You. No one else."

~ * ~

Thomas walked through the crowd of mourners. He approached the closed casket with his hands tucked into his coat pockets. He wanted to see her one last time. He wanted to say good-bye but instead all he could do was stare blankly at the large wooden box before him. Something inside of him gave. Something refused to believe she was gone.

A hand fell gently onto Thomas's shoulder.

Thomas turned and found Anthony standing right beside him.

"Thank you for coming," said Anthony.

Thomas stared blankly into Anthony's eyes. Lost in the light blue reflection, without words or thoughts to express how he felt. Thomas found other memories coming back to him…

~ * ~

Michelle sat in a booth across from Thomas. She fidgeted with her drink and seemed to be on the verge of tears.

"Anthony's going to stop seeing her," Michelle said. "He's going to stop and we're going to work everything out, Thomas."

"Is that what you want?" Thomas asked.

"Yes. That's what I want. I want Anthony and I to be a married couple again."

"Okay, then. I can't do anything else. If this is what will make you happy, then I hope it works out. I want the best for you," Thomas said.

"Thank you," Michelle said as she wrapped her arms around Thomas. "I love him too much, Thomas."

"I know."

"Thank you for being such a good friend." Michelle kissed his cheek. Thomas felt her soft lips brush his course, stubbled face.

He grabbed her hands and gently squeezed them. "I know you'll always love Anthony. He's a lucky man. I hope he'll realize how lucky he is to have you." Thomas pulled Michelle close. His face almost touching hers. "I'll never give up on you though. I want you to know that."

"I do." She kissed him. "Goodbye, Thomas."

Her hands slid from his hold. He stood still and watched her leave. The intoxicating taste of her lingered on his lips.

~ * ~

"Thomas?" Anthony asked.

"Sorry…" Thomas woke from his daydream only to find his life a nightmare. He was back at the funeral home.

"Thank you for coming, Thomas," Anthony repeated.

"Thank you. I'm … sorry. I'm sorry for your loss, Anthony." Thomas extended his hand.

"Thank you." Anthony shook Thomas's hand.

~ * ~

Thomas tossed and turned in his sleep. Dreams tormented him like a breaking fever. Michelle was out of his life. He sat up in bed and reminded himself that she was gone.

Tears filled his eyes and he felt his world spin out of control. He wanted to drink, he wanted to die, he wanted to vanish into thin air. He wanted it to be over but the only thing that made any sense was the thought that Michelle never gave up on him.

He looked out of his bedroom window into the midnight sky. A full moon hung from the clouds and several miles away in a lonely cemetery, Michelle lay in a coffin. He wondered how long it would take for her friends to move on. How long would it take Anthony to find another woman and make her his wife? How long would it take the rest of the world to forget someone as amazing as Michelle?

Thomas was no longer weeping. He was angry.

He rummaged through the pile of clothes that lay on the floor. He found a pair of jeans and a dark tee-shirt. He got dressed and raced out of the house and into his car.

~ * ~

Thomas parked his rusty Camaro along a side road beside Brooke's Cemetery. He popped the truck and pulled out a shovel. He threw the shovel over the fence, into the cemetery, and then jumped the fence.

Thomas grabbed the shovel and raced through the rows of graves until he found her grave site.

He thrust the shovel into the ground as hard as he could and picked up a mound of dirt. He tossed the shovel full of earth to the side and started again.

Thomas dug with all his might until he reached the vault that encased the coffin. He hit the lock on the vault with one hard blow.

Nothing happened.

Thomas swung again.

The lock did not budge.

He ran back to where he parked the car, jumped the fence and found a tire iron in the trunk. Thomas returned to the grave. He hit the lock with the tire iron once and then slid the tire iron between the lock.

He pulled.

The lock didn't move.

Thomas pulled once more. He used all the strength he had left in his body. The muscles in his back tightened as much as they could. His legs pushed with all their might while his arms curled and burned.

The lock snapped.

Thomas lifted the vault door and found Michelle's coffin.

He dropped down into the ditch and pulled the lid open.

Michelle's body lay motionless inside.

Thomas wept. He lifted her torso up and cradled her head in his arms. Tears rolled down his cheeks.

Thomas leaned in and kissed her lips.

Michelle opened her eyes. "Thomas?"

He pulled back.

"Thomas, what happened?" she asked.

"You ... you died."

"What?"

"You were in an accident and didn't make it."

"But I'm here with you," she said.

"I know."

"How?"

"I don't know. You never gave up on me. I guess I couldn't stand the thought of giving up on you. You pulled me out of my own hell. If I truly loved you, then I needed to return the favor."

She hugged him.

~ * ~

Thomas flipped the steak over in the frying pan. Hot grease jumped from the pan, burning his arm. He looked over in the back corner of the restaurant at the girl with the half crooked smile waiting for him. He smiled and Michelle waved back.

Thomas had another hour left before he could go home to the woman he was destined to be with. He returned to his responsibilities in the kitchen with a smile on his face. After all, love doesn't die. It only sleeps until it's awoken by someone courageous enough to believe when the rest of the world has forgotten.

No Pain

Whoever thought that there was gain in pain was on crack. A nut job of a psycho. Yeah, the saying should be no pain, no gain ... no brain.

You ever have a boss or a coach like that? A little drill sergeant of a man spewing out that sickening mantra while you're running suicides in 110 degree heat. Meanwhile, he's sitting in the shade.

"No pain, no gain boys," he'd say.

You'd like to tell him off, but your mouth's been welded shut because your body can't produce any form of water yet alone, saliva.

"You boys are looking good. There's not a single quitter on this team."

No, shit coach. It's cause anyone that's stopped running is dead. Or has burst into flames by now.

Coach Bignudz was the guy I'm talking about. He was my high school football, basketball and baseball coach. If it had a ball in it, he coached it. I think he also taught an art class. I'm not sure. No one who ever had him as a coach wanted him as a teacher. I think we feared he'd make us run suicides in art class.

Anyway, what's this all about, you might ask. What's my point? Well, I have a story to tell. Maybe you'll learn a little about pain, a little about gain. Or maybe you won't. But I have to get it off my shoulders. Besides, it has something for everyone. It's a horror, a comedy, a tragedy and a love story. A love story between a boy, a girl, and a coach.

No, you sick people. It's not that sort of story. Jeezz…

Where to start? Basically, it starts with Coach Bignudz. How can I describe him so you get the full Bignudz experience? Bignudz was a man surrounded by mystery. There've been a lot of rumors about him. I can't even speculate as to what's real, what's exaggerated and what's an all-out lie because if you knew Coach Bignudz, you knew myth.

Some have said he was a good man. That he tried to prep us boys to become men. He was so hard on us because after returning from war he knew what life had in store for young men. What war was he in, you ask? Well, anyone that knew Bignudz would answer, *all of them.*

He was ageless to us. My father had him as a coach and he said Bignudz looked exactly the same then.

Rumors say that Bignudz destroyed the Soviet Empire. That he was the guy who knocked the Berlin wall down. No one ever saw Bignudz eat so there's been speculation that he was actually the only vampire that could survive daylight. Some believed he sold his soul to the devil to get out of prison. A prison where he ate inmates who crossed him. According to this story he was charged with and convicted of war crimes against multiple nations. That landed him eight consecutive life sentences. Three of the eight sentences he out lived.

Some believed he was the devil. That he ruled hell at night and coached during the day.

Others believed he was the only man the devil was afraid of, and after his death, he returned to earth under the condition that he never again go back to hell and make the devil run suicides.

There's been many similar stories and rumors. He was supposedly married at one point but no one knew to what. He was the only man to make Chuck Norris cry. He was Chuck Norris' father. He ate Chuck Norris' father. The list is endless yet nothing could be proven or disproved.

Now, those are the rumors. This is what I saw with my own eyes. Was he a vampire? Was he the devil? I still don't know. He was just the toughest and meanest bastard I ever met.

My last year of high school, our baseball team made State. I was a bench warmer and had the privilege or horror of being a part of that team. The night before our last game a few of the guys partied a little too hard. Several got drunk and two guys, one of whom was my closest friend, Jack, met a couple of girls and ran off with them. Now, the next morning the two guys, Jack included, didn't make it back in time for the game. The other guys who got drunk were still too hungover to play and we lost the championship because of it.

Coach Bignudz went crazy. The Monday morning two days after the game he got the principal to dismiss the entire baseball team from their classes. We were told to meet on the football field ... to run suicides. Now, it's dawned on me that some people don't know what a suicide is. Well, that's when you run from one yard line to the next and back and gradually increase the length of the run as you make your way down the field. You'd have to run to one line, touch it. Then run in the opposite direction to the other yard line, touch it and continue. It's supposed to help with conditioning.

Well, coach was waiting for us on the field with several buckets of baseballs and a bin full of football pads. We were forced into the full football gear, helmet and shoulder pads. Then we had to run suicides. As we finished the first set of suicides Bignudz started pelting us with baseballs from the side lines.

"You boys want to party? Here's your party," Coach Bignudz yelled as he fired off fastball after fastball. "You want to celebrate? Here!" He'd pop the short stop in the head. "You like the fine life? You're all a bunch of little prima donnas." Pop.

I was pelted at least eight times. Not that I was counting but that's how many welts I found on my body the following day.

Toward the end of the session Bignudz got so good at hitting us that he was able to hit three people with one ball. We became a living pinball machine. I kept expecting two things to happen that day. The first was to actually see the word 'tilt' over the goal posts. The second was to die.

My friend Jack got the worst of it. Being our starting pitcher, we had a lot riding on Jack. Boys being boys around girls who are easy tend to not think so clearly. Actually, find one 17 year old who wouldn't throw a championship game for sex and I'll show you an adolescent mutation. I couldn't hate him. Even after the four hours of being pelted by Bignudz, I didn't hate him. He never intended to be late. The girls never told him they were from the next town over and he got lost on the way back. Shit happens. But unfortunately for us, when shit happens, Bignudz happens.

Like I said, Jack got the worst of it. He was hit so many times that day that no one could hate him for our loss. To make matters worse, Jack was in charge of returning the balls to Bignudz when he ran out of baseballs.

After our grueling run, no one had the energy to make it through the rest of the school day. We all went to the office and asked for permission to leave. It was the first time I'd ever seen a complete team allowed to skip the rest of the day and the first time I ever saw a school nurse throw up.

No one told their parents because our parents were scared of Bignudz. My mother saw the welts and pretended like they were pimples. My father had more pity on me because he ran his share of suicides when he was my age.

"This is the last time you're going to have to deal with him," said my father. "Tom, after graduation, you'll go to college and he'll be a fading memory."

"Why doesn't anybody do something about him, Dad?"

"We've tried. Damn those tenured teachers."

After the bruises healed, I took my father's words to heart and found encouragement in knowing that once I graduated, I'd never have to deal with my coach again. I must have felt the way Bignudz felt after outliving the first few life sentences.

The rest of the school year came and went without incident. I didn't play any more sports. Jack, on the other hand, needed an athletic scholarship so he was at the devil's mercy. He stuck it through and survived the rest of the year intact.

A week after graduation Jack called me up. The tone in his voice should have given me enough of a clue. I should have hung up. But as a friend, I couldn't.

"I need a favor, Tom … I'm in big, big trouble."

"What sort of trouble are we talking about?"

"Bignudz sort of trouble."

"That is not what I want to hear."

"Please, Tom. I need you to help me."

Although we were speaking over the phone, nearly nine miles away from one another, I could still taste the fear spilling from my friend's mouth.

I picked Jack up and he preceded to tell me about one of either the gutsiest or dumbest pranks ever pulled. Jack and a few of the other guys decided to tar and feather Bignudz's car. I instantly got an image of Bignudz driving around in a Chevy that resembled a giant chicken. I had to give them credit for creativity.

"Everything was going well until one of the guys decided to leave Bignudz a message," Jack said. "He made a giant scarecrow, dressed him up to look like Bignudz, and set it on fire. He spilled a lot of gas, dousing the scarecrow and accidentally set not only the scarecrow, but the car on fire as well."

"No. You're kidding."

"I wish I was because Bignudz came outside to see what was going on. We all ran but since I was one of the few trying to put out the fire, he saw me."

"You sure?"

"Tom, he looked right at me. I thought he'd call the cops or call my parents but instead, he called me. He's threatening to go to every college that's offered me any financial aid and tell them how I screwed up our state championship. He's even going to lie and say that I have a drug problem and that he's suspected me of using steroids."

"What are you going to do?" I asked.

"I have to talk to him. I don't know what else to do. I'll offer to pay for his car. I'll offer him whatever savings I have but if he ruins my chances of going to school, I'm history. I've finally found something scarier than Bignudz."

~ * ~

I left my father a note explaining that Jack and I needed to talk to Bignudz and if we were never heard from again to contact the local authorities. I speculated that our remains could be found buried in either one of the school's sport's fields, Bignudz's backyard or inside Bignudz's intestinal track. I also made it a point to tell him that I loved him and Mom dearly and that I once took twenty dollars from Mom's purse when I was eleven-years-old and felt guilty about it ever since.

~ * ~

We drove in silence to Bignudz's house. I imagined the feeling ripping through my gut was probably the same that a man on death row feels taking his final steps toward the death chamber. My only comfort was in the knowledge that I was here because of Jack and as messed up as this may sound, I knew Jack would be dead before me.

We pulled into Bignudz's driveway. Our coach's charred Chevy looked like an overdone mutant turkey.

I chuckled. Hey, the guys were creative. Like I said, I have to give them that.

Jack and I walked to the front door. I tried to stop my limbs from shaking but couldn't because with every step I took, something in the back of my mind kept yelling, *Dead man walking.*

Jack rang the doorbell.

I think I shit myself a little.

The door opened with Bignudz on the other side.

If I didn't shit myself earlier, I did then.

"What do you two want?" Bignudz asked.

"I need to talk to you coach," Jack said.

"We don't have anything to talk about."

"Please," Jack said.

Bignudz stepped outside and closed the door behind him. "What do you want?"

"I know I messed up and I'm sorry. I'll pay for all the damages myself," Jack explained.

I was here as a witness and to give any emotional support I could but I sure as hell didn't want to get involved. So, I silently watched Bignudz while Jack tried to set things straight. It looked like Bignudz was getting more and more angry the more Jack spoke. A vein in Bignudz's forehead began to pulse.

"I'll do whatever you need me to do to fix the car," Jack said.

The vein in Bignudz' forehead seemed to be screaming at Jack. I couldn't believe it.

"It's not fair for you to ruin my chances at getting into a good school," Jack said.

"Not fair?" Bignudz asked but part of me believed it was the vein in his head that actually bellowed out the question. "Not fair?" He stepped forward.

Jack and I fell back.

"You know what's not fair?" Bignudz asked. "A bunch of snot nosed kids, ungrateful for the opportunities they've received." He moved toward us.

"We've been grateful," Jack replied.

"Grateful?" Bignudz grabbed Jack by his shirt collar and pointed. "Look at my car."

Jack turned toward the burnt Chevy.

"Does that look like something someone would do if they were grateful?" Bignudz asked.

"No but—" Jack began.

This must have sent Bignudz over the edge because he backhanded Jack, sending him flying into the yard.

"I'll show you, grateful." Bignudz raced after him with a series of blows.

Jack tried to defend himself.

"You disrespectful sack of shit!" Bignudz screamed as he laid into my friend.

"Stop it!" I yelled. "Stop it."

"Shut up," Bignudz replied.

Jack curled up into a ball.

Bignudz kept hitting him.

I had to do something. He was going to kill my best friend. I raced over and tried to push Bignudz off of Jack. "Leave him alone."

Bignudz turned and threw a right cross that somehow connected with both of my eyes.

I stumbled back and fell.

"Shut the hell up," Bignudz demanded.

I think I passed out. I'm not sure. I know there was a passage of time I was not aware of because the next moment Jack was no longer in the yard but in the middle of the road. I don't know if he'd crawled there hoping to escape our killer coach or if Bignudz was trying to sweep the street with him. Bignudz must have also run out of curse words in English because he was yelling at Jack in a language somewhere between Spanish and Russian.

Jack needed help.

I grabbed a shovel Bignudz left in his front yard and ran out into the street.

"Leave him alone." I swung the shovel as hard as I could. It slammed into Bignudz's face.

He turned and looked at me.

I shit myself once more. Then I swung the shovel again.

It smashed into his jaw.

I swung again. Then again, and again. I kept hitting him with all I had. Something happened to me. I think it was all those years being tortured by Bignudz, knowing that everyone else who was coached by him received the same hell. It made me snap and I kept swinging. I thought of all the people who were forced to run suicides in 130 degree heat. People like my father and his father and his father.

"Thomas … stop." Jack grabbed the shovel and pulled it away from me.

Bignudz lay motionless on the street.

I started to cry.

"What have you done?" Jack asked. His face was battered and bloody.

"I don't know," I said.

"I … I think you killed him," he said.

"Are you sure?"

Jack searched for a pulse in Bignudz's neck. "I can't feel anything."

"Jack, he's not breathing."

Jack collapsed beside me.

"What am I going to do? I'm in trouble. Oh, God. What have I done?" I shook my head. "What have I done? I'm in trouble. So much trouble."

"No, *we're* in trouble," Jack said.

I rocked back and forth, lost in despair.

"We've got to hide the body," Jack said.

"What?"

"We've got to hide Bignudz."

"Can't we just go to the cops?" I asked.

"Tom, think about it. I burned his car to smithereens. He threatens me and we both show up at his doorstep where you proceed to beat him to death with a shovel."

He had a point. I couldn't argue with the logic. I looked up at him. "Jack?"

"Yeah?"

"Will you help me bury Bignudz?"

~ * ~

As we drove to a secluded area just outside of town, I asked Jack if we should worry about any witnesses but Jack made the observation that all the homes near Bignudz's were vacant. Who would want Bignudz as a neighbor?

We found a hidden trail in the woods and pulled Bignudz from the trunk. We carried him deep into the woods. Bignudz's eyes were open and staring at me. Even in death, the man was scary as hell.

Jack and I took turns digging Bignudz's grave. When we created a pit large and deep enough to hide his body, we took a break and then started digging once more. We spent three hours working as hard and as fast as we could. My hands blistered over and I still kept digging.

After we buried Bignudz, Jack and I collapsed into my car and sat still for what could have been hours. We tried to wrap our heads around what had happened. I felt guilty, upset, angry and hurt all at once.

Maybe Jack sensed what I felt or maybe he was dealing with similar feelings but he turned to me and said, "It's not our fault. You were protecting me. He would have beaten me to death if you had let it go on."

"What now?" I asked.

"We forget about all this. We put it behind us and move forward with our lives."

I turned the key and started the engine. Jack was right. We needed to move forward. I put the car into drive and slowly pulled away from the woods. I stared in my rearview mirror at Bignudz's final resting spot. As the woods faded into darkness, I kept watch. Just in case.

"Holy shit!" Jack yelled.

"What?" I turned toward him.

Jack shook as he pointed ahead of us.

I followed his trembling hand and outstretched finger to the center of the road.

In the center of the road, Bignudz stood before us.

"Gun it!" Jack said.

I floored the accelerator and crashed into him. His body rolled over the car, thudding against the metal exterior.

I stared in my mirror in shock as Bignudz stood once more and gave us the finger.

I stopped, popped the car in reverse and hit Bignudz once more.

He rolled over the car and began crawling toward us.

I pressed the gas, driving back several yards and then sped forward as fast as I could.

"What are you doing?" Jack asked.

"Finishing this guy."

"He can't die. The fucker can't die."

"We'll see about that," I said as I aimed the car straight at Bignudz.

We connected.

Bignudz flew over the car and bounced on the street a few times before he stopped moving.

Jack and I stopped the car, jumped out of the vehicle and inched our way to him.

"Is he dead?" Jack asked.

"I don't know." I grabbed a fallen branch from a nearby tree and poked him with it. "He's not moving."

"You think he's dead now?"

"I thought he was dead the first time I killed him."

"Damn, what are we going to do now?"

"Re-bury him."

~ * ~

We spent the rest of the night splitting our time redigging our original grave and standing guard over Bignudz. I wondered if I should have driven a stake through his heart but the thought of Bignudz bursting into flames like I've seen in countless vampire movies was too much for me. After killing him with the shovel, burying him alive and then running him over three times, followed by a second burial, I hoped we were safe.

~ * ~

Jack and I reached town by morning. We had spent the drive in speechless awe of Bignudz. The man was a wonder. If I told you I wasn't expecting him to jump out at any moment, and eat both our hearts, I'd be lying. However, as we neared home my fear of Bignudz subsided. At least my fear of him returning and seeking revenge on us in this life. In the next, I wasn't sure but in this one, I was safe.

~ * ~

Jack and I said little of our Bignudz experience during the summer. We'd, at times, wonder what the others had heard of Bignudz's disappearance. Several rumors went around town that summer and none involved two students killing him and disposing of the body, twice. So, we felt safe. At least, for the time being.

~ * ~

As summer neared its end, Jack and I grew distant. It's not like I personally didn't like Jack. I've always felt he was one of my best friends. After all, he did help me bury our coach, twice. That sort of loyalty doesn't come around too often in a lifetime. We shared a dark secret and every time I saw Jack, I didn't see him playing on the field and winning ball games for us. I saw him burying our couch in the woods in the middle of the night. Hell, if that's how I saw Jack, I could only imagine how he saw me. After all, I was the one who hit Bignudz with the shovel and ran him over three times. I'm sure the feelings were mutual.

~ * ~

When summer ended, we went our separate ways. Jack received a full ride to a good school. I went to another college far, far away. I think we both wanted to put things behind us. The last I heard, Jack was doing well and was one of the school's top athletes.

I threw myself into my studies and tried to lose myself in schoolwork and campus life. I still thought about our dark secret now and then. It still haunted me. To be honest, it's a difficult thing to explain to a dorm full of guys why you wake up in the middle of the night covered in sweat and yelling Bignudz. To say I was a bit of an outcast in the dorm was an understatement.

~ * ~

As time went on, I found myself hiding out in the study hall. It was there that I met Dawn. She was a fellow studyholic who spent nearly as much time in the study hall as I did. We gravitated toward one another and love slowly formed. I think I knew I was in love with her when I no longer had nightmares of Bignudz that would wake the whole dorm.

School neared an end. I proposed and she accepted. We both got jobs right after graduation and we saved for a wedding. Saving was easy because Dawn didn't want a large ceremony. She had few family members that I knew of. In fact, she hardly spoke of her family so, she wanted a wedding that was more for us.

~ * ~

As time passed and the wedding neared, I wondered if I should tell Dawn what Jack and I did to our coach. I questioned myself over and over again. I broke down and called Jack.

"It's in the past," he told me. "Don't ruin the rest of your life because of something that happened so long ago."

Jack made sense. I needed to move on and let go of what happened. This was something that was a part of my past. Dawn was my future.

~ * ~

Our wedding day neared. I was to meet Dawn's entire family for the first time. Till then I had only met her mother. I went to the airport with Dawn to pick up her father. As I stood in the airport's lobby with Dawn and saw her wave to an old familiar face, I shit myself once more. Dawn's father was Bignudz. I watched him hug Dawn and I passed out.

When I awoke, Bignudz shook my hand with a grip that nearly broke all my fingers. I drove him back to our house with one eye on the road and the other on Bignudz. I expected him to kill his daughter at any moment just to show me he meant business before coming after me. That never happened.

~ * ~

In the days before the wedding, I expected Bignudz to kill me in my sleep. I couldn't rest. Two days before the wedding, I gave up and accepted my fate. He'd attack me when he so chose.

~ * ~

The day of the wedding, Bignudz took me aside. I thought this was the moment. This was the end.

Bignudz grabbed my arm and said, "Don't hurt my daughter and don't fuck with me."

That was all. Nothing else. We were married. Bignudz never mentioned anything to me about our little incident. I don't know if it's because he loves his daughter so much or if he's only waiting till she's either tired of me or heaven forbid, passes before I do. I guess I'll never find out until that day comes. Until then I pray to God Bignudz forgives me because I don't think Jack wants to help me bury him a third time.

Damn it, I should have driven a stake through his heart when I had the chance.

Divided

"I have to go out." Jason said.

"Why?" Anna asked.

"I just do. Need some fresh air." He closed the door behind him and left their one bedroom apartment. He walked down Rosemary Avenue and then headed east on Okeechobee Boulevard.

The night air was humid and warm. The ocean breeze coming from the island was the one thing that made West Palm's summer nights tolerable. Jason continued on Okeechobee. He passed the downtown buildings that stretched high above and tried to ignore them by walking faster.

He made it to the bridge that connected West Palm to the island of Palm Beach and began to cross. He glanced behind him at West Palm's version of a skyscraper and stopped.

A roar came from underneath him. He glanced over the rail and saw a speed boat pass under the bridge. He leaned against the rail and felt part of it give. He touched the handrail again and a large chunk of metal broke off. He pushed the metal once more and other pieces of steel cracked off. A chain reaction started and flakes of metal crumbled all around him. Then, not only was the metal breaking away, so was the concrete. Jason expected to fall but noticed something was underneath the metal and stone. The bridge was not crumbling apart but breaking away from other steel and brick.

Jason lay frozen as a second bridge grew out of the first. Within moments, steel cables flew overhead, concrete gave way to bricks below and in what seemed to happen in a few blinks, Jason found himself standing in the center of the Brooklyn Bridge. He turned and realized that the sky line was not West Palm's but instead, New York's. The East River was below and Brooklyn before him.

~ * ~

Jason continued to walk. He made his way through Henry Street in Brooklyn Heights until he found the Hotel St. George. He stepped into the lobby. Ralph, the security guard, opened the door.

Jason went to the elevator and pressed the button for the seventh floor. The elevator moved and when the doors opened, he turned right. A few yards away he found room 752. He paused at the door. Not sure what to do, he waited then knocked.

"Who is it?" asked a woman.

It was her voice. A tear rolled down Jason's cheek. "It's me," he said as he wiped his face.

"Come in."

Jason opened the door and found Nancy smiling on the other side.

"What took you?" she asked.

"I … I decided to walk."

~ * ~

"Jason. Jason, wake up," Anna said.

"What is it?" he asked.

"You're going to be late for work."

"Damn it." Jason raced out of bed. He threw on the clothes that were closest to him.

"You're going to wear those?" Anna asked.

"It's either last night's clothes or last week's. What would you rather I wear?"

"Okay, but we're doing laundry when you get home tonight. By the way, how late were you out last night?"

Jason paused and thought about Nancy.

"Jason?" Anna asked.

"What?"

"Last night?"

"I don't remember."

"Where'd you go?"

"Brooklyn."

Anna laughed.

~ * ~

Jason was trapped by rush hour traffic. His car idled and when it moved it did so for only a few feet. He clutched the steering wheel with all his might and then let go as if his squeezing might somehow force the car in front of him to move an extra foot or two.

He looked up. I-95 was a parking lot. There must have been an accident further up the road. He fumbled with the radio until a rock station emerged from all the morning talk shows and static. The last few chords to The Rolling Stone's *Satisfaction* finished up. Jason returned to choking the steering wheel.

The first notes from James Blunt's *High* followed *Satisfaction.* As Blunt's lyrics began, the steering wheel in Jason's hands crumbled to dust. The world around him broke open. The rush hour scene fell apart and beneath it sprouted a small dance studio in Midtown Manhattan. Jason became an audience member sitting in a wooden chair, watching a dance class. Nancy performed to Blunt's lyrics. "Beautiful dawn…"

Jason tuned out the song and the rest of the dancers in the class. He only observed Nancy. She moved unlike any other woman he'd ever known. He couldn't tell if it was the fact that she was six feet tall or that she'd been a classically trained dancer from a young age but there was a fluid grace she naturally held. Maybe it was a mix of both.

Blunt's last lyrics finished with … "getting high." Nancy slowly moved down to the ground. She ended resting on her knees and with her back arched and shoulders touching the floor.

The audience around Jason erupted with applause. He clapped but, just for Nancy.

She rose with a smiled directed at him.

He stood still clapping.

She made her way to him.

"What did you think?" she asked.

"Amazing," he replied.

"It's only a practice class, Jason. I'm not expecting to be that good."

"Well, you are. I could watch you forever."

"You're only saying that because you have to." She kissed him.

"No, I'm not. I don't think I'll ever get tired of watching you dance."

He went to kiss her again but a car horn blared behind him. The dance studio, Nancy, and the rest of New York crumbled. From its remains grew a busy highway in Florida and Jason found himself back in his Pontiac Grand Am being cursed at by the guy behind him for not moving up ten more feet.

~ * ~

Jason arrived at work half an hour late. He snuck into his office and hoped no one noticed. Once at his desk, he closed his eyes, took in a deep breath and waited as he felt the world around him crack apart.

He opened his eyes when he felt his chair rumble and shake. Jason was no longer in an office but inside a subway car. The train vibrated on the tracks.

"Umm. Can't wait to get home," Nancy said. She grabbed his hand and squeezed.

He leaned into her. "I can't either."

The subway car came to a stop. Jason and Nancy exited the car. Their hands entwined and their bodies moved as one. They made their way up the stairs and out of the subway station.

The bracing, winter-night air stopped them when they reached street level.

"Come here." Nancy said. She pulled him close. "You're going to get sick." She searched through her purse and found a brightly colored rainbow scarf.

"I don't think it matches my outfit," Jason said.

"I don't care." She wrapped the scarf around his neck and kissed him. She moved forward, holding his hand.

Jason stopped and watched her move. She was beautiful. New York seemed to bow down to her.

"Are you coming?" she asked.

"Yeah, just wanted to look at you."

A phone rang and the world before him crumbled. Jason found himself back in his office. The smell and frost of New York's winter died and in its place was the scent of an office Jason would have rather forgotten.

~ * ~

"Hey, don't forget we have laundry to do tonight," Anna said.

Jason closed the door to their apartment and placed his things down on the nearby desk.

"I can't right now," he replied.

"Why?"

"If you don't mind, I just need to get out. I … I need some exercise or something."

Jason stepped through the living room, passed Anna in the kitchen and entered the bedroom. He rummaged through a dresser and found a pair of shorts and a tee-shirt.

"Jason, what's wrong?" Anna asked. She entered the bedroom and waited for a reply.

Jason finished changing. He glanced around the room's floor. "Where are my sneakers?"

"Jason, are you going to answer me?" she asked.

"Damn it, I just want to find my sneakers and go for a run. Why can't I do that?"

"You're upset. I want to know what's going on."

"I'm stressed. I want to go out for a run. That's all." He turned a couple of times in the room. "Damn it. Why can't I find anything in this apartment?"

"They're probably in the closet."

He looked in the closet and found a pair of beat up Adidas waiting for him in the corner. He put his shoes on and walked past Anna. "Thanks. Sorry, I'm upset. I just need to think about some things."

Jason left the apartment, jogged down Rosemary Avenue and headed east on Detura Street. When he hit Flagler he noticed the large buildings in the downtown area and turned south. He began to sprint as if the buildings were trying to catch up to him. He ran under the Okeechobee bridge, then ran even faster. His heart raced like never before. He wondered when this world would break apart and the next emerge. What scent, song, or even thought would trigger the next change. He pushed his body harder. He passed people on Flagler but moved so quickly that their faces were all a blur. He worried that someone's smile would bring about a change or that the perfume from a woman sitting on a bench could make the world he now lived in crumple to pieces. Jason pushed on until he felt like his heart was going to explode. He stopped just as Flagler turned into a residential area where the Intracostal Waterway was no longer on his left. He paused before a palm tree, dropped down in the grass and leaned back against the tree. When his back touched the trunk, the tree crumbled.

Jason fell back. He closed his eyes and when his back hit the ground, he found himself lying in Central Park. Nancy sat beside him.

"Here, try some." She held up an ice cream sandwich and offered him a bite.

He shook his head.

"Why? I thought you liked these."

"I do, it's just that…"

She grabbed his hand. "What's wrong?"

"I don't know. I don't know anymore." He looked at Nancy, then over the park. It was spring and in the world's biggest city, a large patch of green with a few lakes, a boat house, a carousal, Poet's Walk, a castle, a zoo and a maze of walkways and hills, one found heaven. Whoever designed the city knew that at the heart of it all, business meant nothing without pleasure. That life was nothing without love. There was no other place on earth like Central Park. He looked into Nancy's eyes and knew there was no other woman like the one before him.

~ * ~

Jason opened the door to the apartment on Rosemary Avenue. Anna waited inside. She sat on the sofa and watched TV.

"How was your run?" she asked.

"Long. Too long."

"Are you okay, Jason?"

"I don't feel so well, Anna."

She rose to his side. "What's wrong?"

"I don't know."

She seized his hands. "My God, you're ice cold."

"Anna, I have to tell you something."

"What? What is it?"

"I'm trapped between two worlds. I don't know where I belong."

"What do you mean?"

"I don't know anymore. I don't know where I belong. I don't know where I'm supposed to be."

Jason's chest began to ache. He clutched the area where the pain came from.

"What's wrong?" Anna asked.

"I don't know." He removed his shirt. The center of his chest cracked.

"Oh God," gasped Anna.

Jason held his chest once more. The cracks grew. Each one splintered away and lead to more breaks until Jason crumbled into nothing.

Lost Pup

Travis heard the whimper as he fished the house keys from his coat pocket. He paused and listened. The whimper came softly, carried by the slight October breeze that tiptoed through the night.

"Who … who's there?" he asked.

The cry came again.

Travis made his way around the side of the house. Underneath the rose bushes his wife, Angela, had planted a year ago, huddled a lost puppy.

He reached down for the small dog. "What mess have you got yourself into stranger?"

The puppy stared up at him with a lost desperation. Travis looked away. He did not want to empathize with the dog's sorrow. Thorns dug deep into Travis's arms. Too numb to feel, he pulled the dog out from under the roses without as much as a single flinch. He cradled the dog with one arm.

"How long have you been trapped underneath those bushes?" Travis opened the front door and was shocked by the silence that waited inside.

"I'm going to need to get used to—"

He stopped. There was no need to finish the rest of the sentence. There were things he did not want to think about. Things that would have to come later. Much later.

He looked down at the dog in his arms. "You must be hungry. Let's see what we can find for you to eat."

~ * ~

The refrigerator was bare. "Honey, where…" Travis stopped. *She was getting groceries. There's nothing in here because it was all in the car when…*

Numbness set in.

Travis looked down at the pup and whispered, "Not much to eat. Seems like I'm a very bad host."

He set the dog down at his feet. "Let me see what I can scrounge up." Toward the back of the refrigerator he found a Tupperware container with leftover turkey. Travis shredded the larger pieces of poultry by hand and set the container down in front of the pup. "Here you go."

The phone rang in the other room. Travis left the dog in the kitchen and answered the phone.

"Hello?" Travis asked.

"Travis, baby are—"

"Mom, I'm fine."

"Honey, we just heard the news. I'm so sorry."

So sorry? Why does everyone have to say those two words?

"Travis?"

"Yeah, mom."

"Your father and I could come—"

"No, mom. Please. I don't need the two of you down here."

"Honey, we know what you must be going through and—"

"Mom, please," Travis replied. "There are a lot of things that I have to do around here."

"We could help."

"Thank you but I'd feel better dealing with everything myself."

"Honey, are you sure—"

"Thanks for calling, mom. I have to go."

"Okay. We love—"

"Bye mom." Travis dropped the receiver and caught his breath. *They mean well. Can't be mad at them. They're only trying to help. Can't be mad. Can't be mad at anyone.*

An image of Angela flashed through his thoughts. Her brown locks of hair dropping to her shoulders. Her curls would bounce whenever she moved her head a certain way. Her smile seemed like a secret only shared with him.

The day he lost his job she stayed up with him all night. Angela kept him company as he reworked a seven-year-old resume. He remembered how she leaned over and kissed him on the cheek. "You're always holding things in," she whispered. "It will eat you alive if you don't find a release."

Travis shook his head. The numb feeling came again. He made his way back to the kitchen. The puppy had not touched his food.

"Not hungry?" Travis asked.

The pup glanced up.

"No, I guess not," Travis said.

~ * ~

A day had vanished. A new one begun. Travis met with a funeral director that a friend of Angela's had recommended. The man was short, balding, and wore round spectacles. The funeral director looked more like an aging college professor than a mortician. The man walked Travis through all of the steps and details. Plans for the service were settled upon and a visitation scheduled.

"I'm so sorry for your loss," the funeral director said as he escorted Travis outside his office.

Travis, lost in a daze, did not reply.

"Sir, are you okay?" the funeral director asked.

"Oh, sorry … I was … I was just thinking. I have a small dog at home and I need to stop by the pet store today. The poor thing hasn't eaten in a couple of days."

"If there's anything at all we can help you with, please call."

"Oh … okay."

~ * ~

Travis entered his house with a small bag under his arm. "I brought you some food," he said. Travis placed the bag on the kitchen counter and pulled out a box of Puppy Chow. Behind Travis came a scratching sound.

He turned.

A full grown dog stared up at him. The dog had the same desperation in his glance that Travis had seen in the puppy's eyes when he pulled him from the rose bushes. Travis looked around for the puppy, then realized this was the same dog.

Travis went numb.

"I brought you something to eat," Travis said. "Something better than that leftover turkey." He poured the dog food into a bowl and placed the bowl on the kitchen floor.

The dog looked down at the food, sniffed it and then walked away.

Travis looked over at the phone in the living room. There were calls he needed to make. People who needed to know about the services for Angela. He looked down at the bowl of dog food at his feet. "Yeah, I guess I'm not hungry either."

~ * ~

The viewing began early in the afternoon. Friends made their way to Travis with the kindest of intentions. Each paid their respects but Travis realized few seemed to connect with him.

Softly spoken exchanges littered the funeral home.
"Is he okay?"
"God, can you imagine what he—"
"Terrible, terrible…"
"Has Travis said anything about…"
"Married eight years and now—"

Travis heard the whispered concerns but paid no mind. His wife lay only a few feet from him, but Travis could feel nothing. Instead, his concerns were with a stray dog that kept him company at night and apparently had no appetite.

~ * ~

The house was still, frozen in time like an old black and white photograph long forgotten. Travis sat on the couch and stared blankly into the darkness. There were no sounds of a woman's footsteps, no soft whispers or slight sighs. No noise to let Travis know that he was not alone. The only sound came from the kitchen as a dog curled up around a full plate of food.

Travis looked over at the animal. Its extremities had lengthened and its body had almost doubled in size. The animal looked more like a large wolf than the pup Travis had first found.

"We bury her tomorrow," Travis said. He looked at the plate before the animal. A fried two-pound piece of steak was left untouched by the dog.

"We bury her tomorrow and you're still not hungry."

~ * ~

Angela's casket was lowered into the ground. Travis didn't blink. He stood with the crowd of mourners. Tears fell from the eyes of longtime friends who now seemed like strangers. Travis stood frozen, his face held the expression of a marble sculpture. For a second Travis thought of the first day he met Angela. She was reading a book in the park under an old elm tree. He remembered the yellow summer dress she wore as she looked up and smiled.

He chased the rest of the memory away before it could fill him.

The crowd began to disperse. Travis's mother turned to him. "Honey, would you like us to come home with you?"

Travis stared at an elm tree in the distance.

"Son, we're planning on staying at least a week," said Travis's father. "We can stay longer if you need us."

"We'll stay as long as you need us," echoed his mother.

Travis said nothing. The memories of Angela came back. He thought about all that he had and all he had lost. He thought about his broken promises and about a future that no longer existed. Then, he thought about the dog waiting at home. He remembered how much larger the animal had gotten over night.

"Son?" asked his father.

"I have to get home," Travis said.

"We'll go—" began his mother.

"No, no. I'll be fine," Travis replied.

"We'll be by around…"

"Mom, dad … please. I have to go." Travis hurried past them. His mind racing with memories of the woman he married. The same woman he had just buried.

~ * ~

Travis opened the door to his house.

"Angela," he cried.

Emptiness echoed back.

"Ang … Ange…" Tears streamed down his face. "Oh God Angela. You're right. I do hold too much in."

The door closed behind him.

"I do hold everything in."

He waited and hoped for a reply.

"I held in how much you've meant to me. I've kept my fears from you, my pain from you…"

Travis hoped that the last days were all a dream. That his wife was here in their house and not gone. That her voice would come from a hidden corner of their home, not from a hollow memory in his mind.

"Angela!"

Nothing.

"Angela, I'm so sorry for keeping so much from you. I'll promise never … never to … please. Please Angela, please let this all be a dream. Say something. Let me hear your voice one last time."

Travis waited for a noise.

Several footsteps came from the kitchen.

Travis raced toward the noise.

"Angela!"

Travis stopped. Eye level with him stood an animal that was less dog and more beast. Its legs were the length of Travis's body, its paws the size of a large man's hands. The animal's mouth slightly larger than Travis's face.

Drowned in desperation, Travis discovered the gleam in the animal's eyes and realized it was finally hungry.

Afterward

So, we've arrived at the end. I hope you've enjoyed the ride. Anyway, you may have a few questions for me. Like, why an afterward for this book? Well, let's face it. I write some pretty strange stuff. Some of which probably needs explanation. So, if any story left you wondering what happened or if it peaked your interest and you want to find out a little more about the tale, you can read about it here. The comments for each story are in the same order that you found them in the book. Be warned, if you've skipped ahead to this part of the book, you might spoil the ending to some of the tales.

Of Wolves and Moons
This is one of my favorite stories. It's a tale that flowed out of my imagination so easily and with such energy that it felt like I never wrote it to begin with. Not only was it so easy to write but the narrator's distinct speech and tone was like nothing else I'd written before. Part of me wonders if the Creator threw me a bone that day and made the ghost of a better writer whisper the story in my ear.

I like to use Magic Realism in some of my stories. Sometimes a narration is filled with symbols and metaphors. In *Of Wolves and Moons*, grief and loss transform the father into a wolf. Throughout the tale the father is concerned about his son's own handle on losing his mother. He tries to keep the boy sheltered from such pain and becomes troubled when the boy loses his silver necklace symbolizing innocence. In the end we find that the young boy has a better grip on grief and actually supports his father's own expression of sorrow by being at his side during his transformation.

I know ... a little too deep, but damn it, I like this story.

The Painter

This story was the first piece of fiction that I had published. It originally appeared in *Horror Garage #10*. The tale is about love and addiction. Julian confronts his former lover, Helen, and wants to know why she could never care for him. We discover that Helen is actually heroin and that Julian is going to use her one last time to end his life.

In my experience, certain women have been more of a drug and love more of an addiction. I let that idea blend itself into this story and allowed things go from there. The idea lead me to a forgotten painter and his dark muse.

Waiting

This is one of my favorite short stories because one gets two different emotions depending on the character's perspective. When looking through the narrator's eyes, you experience the retelling of a sentimental love affair but when you start seeing the tale through Ashley's eyes, the emotions change. When Ashley misplaces things to later find them returned or when she falls asleep in one room and then wakes up in another, one realizes the ghost of her fiancé is still taking care of her. This realization changes the whole mood of the tale.

Splitting Up
Originally this story was a play. I began writing fiction through some earlier involvements in theater. This was one of my first one-act-plays. I decided to beef it up with some description but still keep it as bare as possible using dialogue to tell a tale. *Splitting Up* is also one of my first tales where I incorporate the strange and bizarre as a major component of the narrative.

The Meeting
I've been known to have a monstrous appetite. I let my imagination run away with that hunger. When my imagination and hunger returned, they had to enter Over Eater's Anonymous. *The Meeting* came from that encounter.

Found Note
One theme that's come up in my stories is the idea of turning into a monster. This has been one of my own personal fears. In *Found Note*, we enter a place where young boys have to become abusive monsters or they're banished. The narrator chooses to die rather than turn into the monster he's expected to become.

Occupation

I'm sure we've all known at least one person whose house has been broken into. This story comes from the question, what if a burglar broke into a killer's house?

666

The mark of the beast. In *666* we're introduced to beast and his first victim.

Journal Found in Woods

As stated in my explanation of *Found Note*, one of my nightmares is of turning into a monster. I let that fear turn into this story.

The Writers' Group

I've worked with a writer's group called The Bloody Pens for several years. Every few weeks we'd meet and have a different theme or story idea to incorporate into a compilation. *The Writer's Group* came from one of these meetings. One day someone proposed we write a story about a writer's group. This was my response to that challenge.

The Last Song

I took a trip to Seattle, Washington in March of 2010 with a group of college students. I was the advisor for an art club and as part of my duties, I had to chaperone students on trips.

One night I discovered two amazing musicians performing at the Edgewater Hotel. They were a brother and sister group that became one of the highlights of the trip for me. I, like the character James, was captivated by what I saw and heard. One song in particular killed me. I'm always amazed how a singer can spell out everything you've ever felt but can't express in words. That night, I would have given anything to have that same power. So, I created James.

A Father's Warning
Originally, this tale began one way and I intended for it to end differently but then something happened. I thought about my father, who passed away in October 2009 and my emotions brought the story to a completely different place. I thought about how parents try to keep their kids safe in the world and yet, as we grow up, we end up in those exact places we were warned about. I thought of how the love of a parent or their memory can sometimes bring us back to the light. The story revolved around that idea and was also about how we need to find a way to say our final good-byes.

Getting Personal
In this world of computers and the World Wide Web, we've come to a point where love can be found on hundreds of dating sites. I have tried some of these sites myself as have most of my friends. Some people have good results. Others, not so good.

In *Getting Personal*, we find the beginning of a love affair between two unlikely people. I felt like writing a happy ending. In part, to remind readers that not everyone gets eaten by a monster or dies at the end of my stories.

The Fisherman

I like guardian stories. I grew up on the tales of white knights protecting castles and I thought, what if paradise was protected by a single man. After living in Florida for most of my life, I can't imagine paradise not being surrounded by a beautiful beach. With time, a fisherman landed on that beach with a net that would catch all your troubles. This story is one of my favorites because one not only meets this powerful guardian, one meets his predecessor as well, and one gets the idea as to how someone becomes *The Fisherman*.

High Stakes

I, like most of America, got hooked on the Texas Hold'em craze and have won and lost my fair share of games and money. I felt I needed at least one story on gambling. Not only does this story deal with gambling but it deals with another favorite theme, addiction. As I've gotten older, the monsters I once feared as a child died off and were replaced by other creatures altogether. One of the saddest and also most horrifying things you experience is the effect of an addiction on a person you care about.

Passed Out

I wanted to experiment with extremely short fiction. My idea was to create a story that could fit on a business card and be used as a promotional tool. I personally like flash fiction. One of the things that drew me to reading short stories was the ability to take five or ten minutes out of my day to read a quick tale. Short stories give me my fix of fiction without interfering with the other things I have to do in the day.

As Promised

I'm sure we've all run into at least one person claiming to be something they are not. In *As Promised*, we find a guy whose lies have finally caught up to him. After years of pretending to be a writer, a demonic Underwood typewriter arrives at his doorstep and forces him to finally sit down and write.

I'm not like other writers who can spew out prose or poetry with ease. Writing, in my experience, is extremely demanding and can leave me banging my head against the wall when I'm stuck on an idea. When I tell myself that I want to write or when I have a large project to do, I see myself as the narrator in this tale. If I don't make time to write and actually create copy, I see myself as a fraud and expect to find a black Underwood waiting at my doorstep.

Charlie's Invitation

I've reached a point in my life where many of my friends are settling down and getting married. I often wonder if there's ever a former lover at any of these ceremonies. There's always that heightened moment in the wedding when the audience is asked for any reason why the couple should not wed. If there is a reason, it should be known now or never mentioned again. The prankster in me wants to yell out or raise my hand to stop the ceremony, then say, just kidding. I know people would laugh but I fear the wrath of an angry bride with a limited sense of humor.

It's this moment in the ceremony the writer in me lives for. I wonder who's in the audience holding their breath, biting their tongue, or dying on the inside. In this story, I tried to capture a tale about a man having to say good-bye to the woman he still loves. I imagine that final day being one of the hardest he'd ever have to face and in this case, Charlie takes his own life over and over again and yet can't die. It's not until he sees the love of his life walk down the aisle that he is finally able to pass.

Found Doll

I've always been a fan of vampire stories. *Found Doll* was my way of entering the vampire world from a different angle. I started to think about a toy a vampire child would own.

The Letter

This piece of flash fiction jumped into my head one slow afternoon. I started to fantasize about a letter from the future arriving in the mail. I put a horror twist into it and received *The Letter*.

Last Bullet
See the notes for *Passed Out*.

The Tree
As stated in *Charlie's Invitation*, during weddings I often wonder if there's ever a lover in the audience waiting to stop the wedding. In *The Tree*, the ceremony is stopped by the groom because of a tree that calls out to him from a nearby field. When Adam climbs the tree that he and his adolescent girlfriend climbed as kids, he discovers that a heart with both their names now has the word 'forever' written underneath. Adam has been haunted by her memory throughout his life and realizes he'll never forget her.

I also wanted to tell a story about how a certain injustice not only affected one person but many people. The victim in this tale was not only Emily. Everyone else around her suffered as well.

Lostinhorrorhouse.com
I have a friend who loves looking up strange things online. He's had a knack for finding any recorded mutilation or deaths through countless websites that showcase such material. Although I'm a massive fan of horror, I don't like to watch real life tragedy. This story stemmed from countless arguments where my friend has told me to look at something on his computer and I find a corpse staring back at me.

Recovered

This is my take on the old Sleeping Beauty tale. It's a bit more twisted than the original and hopefully it packs a little more punch. In this adaptation, Michelle is dead and is later awoken by her prince. I've also tried to write a story around the idea that love doesn't allow one to give up on the people one cares about.

No Pain

This is one of my first attempts at writing comedy. I've been extremely lucky to have such an amazing cluster of people in my writers group to help me through rough patches. During one meeting someone brought a sheet filled with motivational sayings that were changed for the sake of humor. This writer thought it would be a good idea for us to take one of the sayings and turn it into a story. I got the, 'no pain, no gain,' saying and ran with it. I guess I ran so far that I bumped into Coach Bignudz. Then I was forced to run suicides.

Divided

In life, some of the most difficult times we face are the moments when we're torn between two worlds. For me it's usually when I'm trying to live in the present but part of me is stuck in the past.

In *Divided*, Jason can't let go of the lover he once had and he can't embrace the love and life he currently leads. He's constantly brought back to his past. In the end, it destroys him. For me, the inability to move on and let go of one's past has brought me to these breaking points where, like Jason, we emotionally fall apart.

Lost Pup

Travis finds a small puppy that grows abnormally fast for a dog. The dog's size symbolizes the grief Travis is running from. In the end, Travis breaks down and faces the loss of his wife. He discovers the pup has grown into a monster that's ready to … devour him.

Thank you for the company on our long journey. I hope you've enjoyed the stories and my comments. May we bump into each other soon enough. Until then, may you always have love in your life, courage in your heart, and may those you love always be at your side. I wish you the best.

Sincerely,

Joel Betancourt

About the Author

Joel Betancourt is a Cuban born ceramic artist and writer. His written work has been published in Ceramics Monthly, Active Times Magazine, Pottery Making Illustrated, Horror Garage, and The Palm Beach Post. His debut novel, *Porcelain Doll*, was well received by critics and fans. His ceramic work has been shown in numerous South Florida galleries. He lives in West Palm Beach, Florida.

Note to Reader

Dear Reader,

The publishing world has experienced some massive changes in the last few years. Now, more than ever, authors need your help to ensure their livelihoods. Please support your independent authors by reviewing their work and spreading the word so they can continue to write the stories that keep you entertained. Without readers' comments, reviews, or feedback, new authors cannot thrive in the current publishing climate.

If you've enjoyed this book, please write a review on Amazon. A simple line or two stating that you've enjoyed the work is enough to let others know a story has moved you. Feel free to write a longer review if you like but for those of you who are shy, a sentence or two is incredibly helpful.

Also, please share your experiences with this work of fiction through Facebook, Twitter or any other social media you use. Other like-minded readers will appreciate the information and authors' careers depend on it. In a digital age, word travels further and faster than ever before.

Thank you for your time, your thoughts, and for the chance to entertain you. I hope we meet again.

Sincerely,
Joel Betancourt